THE UNITED FEDERATION MARINE CORPS' GRUB WARS

BOOK 3

DIVISION OF POWER

Colonel Jonathan P. Brazee
USMC (Ret)

Semper Fi Press

Acknowledgements:
I want to thank all those who took the time to offer advice as I wrote this book. A special thanks goes my editor, Abbyedits, and to my beta readers James Caplan and Kelly O'Donnell for their valuable input.

Cover art by Matthew Cowdery
Graphics by Steven Novak

DEDICATION

Stephen J. Riordan III, Commander, USN (Retired)

Surface Line and Navy Air

WWII, Korea, Vietnam

RIP

and

Signalman Second Class Kenneth A. Groth, USNR (Ret)

WWII

DESIGNATED PLANET G8

Chapter 1
Hondo

Coming in too fast, Staff Sergeant Hondo McKeever, United Federation Marine Corps, thought, images of his body crashing and burning onto the planet's surface filling his mind.

Even after two months training in the Klethos podsuit, he still wasn't comfortable with the feeling that he was falling. This was worse than the transit through bubble space—for that part of the journey, he was thankfully drugged into near-stasis. Now, when he needed to be on alert, his body was clean of all little helpers.

Just deal with it.

More than a few Interrecon candidates, many of them super-grunts, had washed out because they couldn't take the mode of transport. Some of those candidates had been so mentally traumatized that they'd not only washed out of ARS, Advanced Reconnaissance Course, but out of the Corps as well.

He looked to his right. Somewhere out there was Ben, but he couldn't pick him out. Which was a good thing. Part of being in recon was remaining unseen, something that would be difficult if they were trailing a flaming torch as they plunged through the atmosphere.

Below him, Hondo could see a large expanse of trees stretching out past the horizon. Supposedly towering 300 meters, he didn't need to get hung up in one. He had to trust his podsuit navigator to get him through a yet-unseen hole in the canopy.

The growing pressure in his bladder was not helping things. The podsuits were never designed for human waste. While in the transit near-stasis, his body wasn't producing any waste to speak of, but now, six hours fully conscious, his bladder screamed for release. He could just let go, of course, but he didn't fancy walking around on a hostile planet reeking of piss.

Come on, McKeever! You're an Interrecon Marine, for God's sake. Forget about your freaking bladder.

Easier said than done, he knew, but he peered below him, trying to see where the navigator was taking him. The ground below had gradually changed from an expanse of blurry green to discernable trees, looking much like a forest on any terraformed world in human space. Only this was not a terraformed world. This had been a *Telorra* planet, belonging to a race long ago exterminated by the Klethos and subsequently taken by the Grubs over 70 standard years ago. The trees below were not oaks or firs but simply alien analogs of Earth trees, cases of parallel evolution.

The awe of what Hondo was about to do broke through his concern about his rate of descent. He was about to be the first human to set foot on this planet, designated G8 by the task force command, parsecs beyond where any human had ever yet ventured. Well, not quite. Scattered throughout this sector of the galactic arm, twenty-four other Interrecon teams were landing on different Grub-held planets. They were part of a concerted effort to gather intel on the enemy, to be proactive rather than reactive in the war. Hondo and Ben hadn't been given any specific mission orders—they were being sent to observe and gather any intel they could. No one knew what tiny piece of information could be used to turn the tide of the war.

All Hondo and Ben knew was that there was a large group of Grubs 30 klicks or so from the DZ. It was their mission to see what the Grubs were doing. Usually, the Grubs moved on from the worlds they conquered, but according to the Klethos, they remained on about 15% of the worlds for no reason yet discernable to anyone. Some, like this one, were very Earth-like while others were barren, rocky balls devoid of life.

Hondo's mind snapped back into reality. He could make out the individual trees now as he plummeted to the ground. What he hated was that, unlike being inserted by duck egg and flying a wing to the surface, in a podsuit, he had no control over his descent; he was just along for the ride. No Marine or soldier had been killed by a podsuit failure—yet. All machines failed sometimes, however, even Klethos machines. He was just about convinced that his podsuit would be the first to crash and burn when he was pushed against the clear front of the suit as it slowed down, the internal dampeners not quite able to handle the change in G-forces. Still 500 meters above the tops of the trees, he started moving laterally before dropping down again, slipping between two forest giants and into a murky twilight, the planet's sun blocked by the heavy foliage.

He breathed a heavy sigh of relief as he slowly descended past the immense bole of a tree, small orange animal life darting around the wrinkled and mottled "bark." The Klethos had eliminated the Telorra from the planet (and from the galaxy, for that matter), but they'd left the lower life-forms alive. When the Grubs took the planet, they'd killed off everything larger than the size of a house cat (according to the Klethos), and the Navy drone in orbit confirmed that there were no larger animals on the planet's surface. If Hondo could have controlled his podsuit, he'd have slowed down to take a better look at the orange critters.

The little guys weren't a threat to him, though, and he shifted his attention to the ground below. As he descended, the trees opened up more than enough to allow Grubs to move between the trunks. Hondo didn't know if they sent out patrols as humans might, but Marines who assumed things were safe rarely lived to collect on their retirements. Hondo checked his M96—he was at 99% power and at a full combat load of 28 rounds. He couldn't fire his weapon through his podsuit, but he wanted to be ready if he came down on some Grub picnic. The ground was deserted, however, as he descended the final twenty meters, coming to a stop on the loamy soil.

Immediately, his podsuit split open at the head, then folded back in on itself over and over until it was a 132 cm by 91 by 68 cube. Hondo still couldn't believe that the 121-kg package was an interstellar space ship, able to transport him through bubble space and get him to his destination in one piece. Some people still thought of the Klethos as primitive, given their love for swords and individual combat, but humanity had nothing that even came close to the podsuits that the Klethos took for granted.

Hondo's first task should have been to secure the area, to make sure there were no Grubs or other dangers around, but biology had no master. First things first. He stepped up to the closest tree trunk, unzipped, and let go. Blessed relief allowed his brain to function again.

Now, I can get on with the mission.

Hondo manhandled his podsuit to the base of a tree, checked his tracker that would lead him back to it, and then inserted his monocle, powering up his display. Ben had already landed, 189 meters to the planetary northwest. Hondo checked his M96 one more time, and with one last scan of the area around him, he stepped off to reunite with his partner.

Marine recon's unofficial motto was "Swift, Silent, and Deadly." The "silent" part of that was easy as he moved under the triple canopy. The dense organic litter absorbed any sound his footfalls might have made as he moved between the huge trunks and around small colonies of what looked to be some sort of bluish, fungus-like growth. There was very little cover to hide his movements, but that would be truer for a lurking Grub. They were simply too large to be able to remain hidden from him.

Ben's avatar hadn't moved from where he'd landed. Hondo wanted to call him to find out if he was OK, but they were on minimal emissions protocol. No one knew just what the Grubs could detect, so the were ordered to avoid transmissions whenever possible. Hondo would reach his teammate soon enough.

Rounding another pseudo-fungus colony, he spotted a tall, slender figure ahead of him, mostly hidden by the bole of a tree. Two left arms were in sight, the lower arm holding a heavy sword, one that could cut through even a Marine PICS.

Hondo positioned himself between the large tree trunk and the figure, then silently approached, careful not to make a sound. He was still 20 meters away when the figure bent to the side, a beaked, raptor-like face taking Ryck into his gaze. Ryck wasn't actually trying to sneak up on him, and now he made no pretense of even trying.

"Hey, Ben. Any Grub sign?" Hondo asked as he reached his partner.

"Negative," the Klethos said. "Nothing at all."

"Well, then, let's go find them."

****

Twenty hours later, Hondo and Ben were crouched at the edge of the forest, looking out over the open field. A klick away, four large Grubs seemed to be watching or guarding what looked to be at least several hundred smaller versions of themselves. Hondo could not contain his excitement. They had to be Grub young. What else could they be?

Capturing a young Grub was the holy grail of the mission. The scientist who briefed the teams were positively salivating over the prospect, and stressed that if the opportunity arose, then the mission should change from discreet observation to direct action. The final call would be to the team leader, of course, but it would be highly, highly recommended—which, in Marine-speak, meant is was pretty much an order.

"What do you think, Ben?" Hondo asked his teammate.

The Klethos' whipcord-thin body was tense as he watched the Grubs. His neck frill twitched, a sure sign that he was excited; "eager" was probably the more accurate term. Hondo had worked extensively with Ben over the last five months, developing procedures for the dual-species teams, and he thought he'd gotten a feel for how the Klethos warrior thought and acted.

"I think that we should see if we can snatch one of them," Ben said, a slight sibilant hiss to his words, another sure sign that he was excited.

For the last hundred-plus years, humans thought that male Klethos were the smaller, meeker members of the race, not suited to be warriors. That was generally true, but only comparatively speaking. The males were still stronger and better fighters than humans. They were also more pragmatic and less prone to take offense, so when the Interrecon teams were proposed, the Klethos suggested that the males be assigned to the teams. Some people thought that this was because they had no confidence in the teams and didn't want to waste "real" warriors. Hondo wasn't sure about that. He'd worked with more than his fair share of Klethos warriors, and while amazing fighters, they could be prickly with their honor and difficult with whom to interface. Not so with Ben. The two had worked very well together. They were a good team.

"There's a shitload of them out there," Hondo said, waiting to hear Ben's response.

"You're the team leader," Ben said. "You come up with a plan, and we'll execute it. You were at the ops-order, though. You know how important this is."

Yes, Hondo did know how important getting a live Grub baby would be, and he was already sure they had to give it a try. But this was the first time that he and Ben were on a live mission, and this was raising the stakes considerably. No human knew how male Klethos would react in combat. Hondo didn't fear cowardice or hesitation from his partner—far from it, in fact. He was worried about the opposite. Over time, Hondo had developed the impression that the male Klethos assigned to Interrecon had somewhat of a chip on their four shoulders, that they reveled in the opportunity to raise the battle standard for their gender. If Hondo was correct in that, then he didn't want Ben to johnwayne it, to forget tactics in an attempt to be a hero.

"Yes, I was at the ops-order, and I heard them. But I have the final say. It won't do us any good to seize one of them if we can't get it off-planet and back to the geeks who'll know what do with it."

He saw the slightest flattening in Ben's neck crest as he flipped his monocle back down, zoomed in to look at the Grubs in the distance. He half expected to hear Ben plead the case for a snatch, but his partner remained silent. Hondo took that as a good sign. He'd wanted to observe Ben's demeanor, his mood, but his decision had already been made. They had to make the attempt.

The only question now was how.

****

Hondo froze in place, his face pressed up against the dirt. Ten meters away, a massive Grub slowly moved forward, its bulk rippling in tiny increments to cover the ground. He wasn't sure how the thing could miss him, but as he watched, it didn't seem to give him any notice. No one seemed to know just what caused a Grub to go into attack mode, although that was a hot topic among Marines preparing to go up against them. Sometimes, Grubs seemed to ignore ground troops or even air fighters until attacked. They continually ignored Navy ships until the ships fired, then three or more of them would merge their light tendrils and knock the ship out of orbit. Other times, they moved in to the attack ground troops or aircraft without provocation.

As the Grub moved past him, Hondo risked raising his head to watch, slowly moving up a hand to rub his nose, and trying to hold in the sneeze that had been building up. The dirt *looked* like Earth-type dirt, it *felt* like Earth-type dirt, but it sure didn't *smell* the same. It had a slightly acrid, tangy smell that had tickled his nasal passages, creating an almost unbearable need to sneeze. Finally, with the Grub 30 meters beyond him, he couldn't hold it in anymore. He pulled up his utility blouse, buried his nose into it, and gave a half-sneeze that did little good. He quickly looked up, but the Grub kept moving away.

The Grub had to have seen him. His utilities had a damper system woven into the fabric that blocked most of his biological signals, but the thing had passed just a few meters from him, and he'd had no concealment. He wondered if the Grubs came in different flavors. These Grubs seemed to be raising the Grub babies. Maybe they weren't built to fight? Hondo couldn't assume that, however. Almost all Terran animals would fight to protect their young. Those in the past that didn't became extinct, and those that did manage to pass on their genes survived. As a basic survival trait, Hondo had to assume that even if these weren't warrior Grubs, they would defend their young. Even if they had some sort of caste system and these Grubs were some kind of nanny-type, then surely there would be warrior-types around to protect them.

At least he thought they must, and he had to assume that to be the case. Underestimating the Grubs could only lead to disaster.

He didn't even have the choice now to abandon their attempt to kidnap a Grub child if things got too hot. He'd broken out his twinned hadron communicator and relayed what they'd found. Some very excited people on the other end had ordered Ben and him to snatch one of the young, then get it back immediately, foregoing the rest of what had been planned as a three-month mission. This was top-priority now.

He wanted to call Ben and ask if he was in position at the far side of the open area, which was partially covered by a purplish moss-like plant, but he held back. He had to trust his teammate, and he didn't want to make any more of a footprint on the planet than he had to. Communications emissions might or might not be picked up by the Grubs, and there was no use taking any chances.

Unnecessary chances, he corrected himself—what they were doing now was one huge risk with little probability of success.

As the Grub continued on its way, the purple moss didn't seem to register its vast bulk. Not so with Hondo. He could swear that the moss polyps were focused on him, swiveling to face him as he moved. But why him and not the far larger Grub? He wondered if the Grubs and the moss might be in some sort of symbiotic relationship, but that would mean that either this was the Grub homeworld, which he knew it wasn't, or they had, well, not terraformed, but *grubaformed* the world. That was all well-beyond his job description, though. He was here to snatch a baby Grub, nothing more. Still, the moss gave him the creeps, and he avoided it, sticking to the dirt.

He kept still until the Grub was 200 meters ahead and rejoining the flock (herd? gaggle?) of babies before he started off again, hugging the dirt in his low crawl, avoiding the patches of moss. He felt very, very exposed, but there was simply no cover anywhere near the Grubs. He didn't have a better route of approach.

His plan—what there was of a plan—was for Ben to wait at the far side of the open area, lying in wait along a swale that they both thought was the logical escape route for the babies. Hondo was going to creep up as close as he could. If a Grub baby wandered close, he'd try to snatch it, but his mission was to fire upon the big

Grubs. He hoped that while he faced them, the others would flee towards Ben, giving the stronger Klethos the opportunity to snatch one as they galumphed by. If they didn't, then hopefully, Hondo would attract enough of their attention so that Ben could rush up and snatch one beneath the slower defenders.

There was a slim possibility that things could work out that way. There were also about a hundred other possibilities that would end in disaster for the team. But after observing the group for the last two days, this was the best he could come up with, and none of the plans suggested by the myriad of folks monitoring the situation seemed any better.

He'd considered waiting for the New Budapest Ranger Battalion that was on its way, but five hours ago, two Grubs had landed, lassoed (for lack of a better term) six of the babies with their light tendrils, and then taken off again. They couldn't take the chance that the rest would be taken before the Rangers could get there, so they'd been ordered to kick off the snatch.

At 140 meters from the nearest Grub, Hondo checked his shielding status. His utilities had been treated with a film of highly conductive cerrostrands, something developed by the Brotherhood. The coating made it easy to overheat during any kind of physical action, but it was designed to shunt a Grub's light tendrils to the side. It didn't make sense to him. If the shielding was conductive, then logic said that it would, well, *conduct* the energy into him. But they colonel who'd given them the brief assured them that it should work.

Should work.

When Colour Sergeant Byron Howell, from Juliette Station, had asked if it had been tested, she was told no. It seemed that Interrecon would be the test subjects. Hondo had gone up against Grubs in only his longjohns before, but he'd feel much more secure in a fully charged PICS.

At about a hundred meters out, he stopped again to observe the Grubs. There were four of the adults and possibly 200 of the babies. Three of the 12-meter-long adults were on the far side of the bulk of the babies while the one that had passed by him had stopped on the near side of them. Hondo wished it was the other way, with three on his side. That might make it more likely that they would move off in Ben's direction. At least this way, he had his target designated.

The adults were on the bare dirt, the babies on the purple moss, barely moving. Something about their movement seemed almost organized. Hondo zoomed in with his monocle, getting a better view of them. The babies were slowly advancing, and it took a moment for him to realize what he was seeing. As the babies moved forward, the moss tops were full of polyps. As the babies passed, the moss they'd been on was much shorter—not flattened, but shorter, as if run over by a lawnmower.

They're eating it! I'm sure of that!

Up until now, no one knew what a Grub ate, or even *if* they ate in the sense that Terran animals and Klethos ate. They had to get the vast amounts of energy they expended in fighting from somewhere, but some xenobiologists calculated that eating organic food simply could not result in enough energy to do what they were able to perform. But here, Hondo could see it. The babies, at least, ate, and it was the purple moss.

This was a vital piece of information, and as there was a very good chance that he was not going to make it back alive, he recorded a full minute of what he saw, then uplinked that back to his command. He waited until he got confirmation, then got back to the mission at hand.

Hondo checked his M96's display. He was still at 99% power and with 29 of the big rounds: 28 in the magazine and one in the chamber. For someone used to carrying thousands of hypervelocity darts, 29 rounds seemed almost criminally negligent. Unlike the 2mm darts, however, the M96 rounds were 46 mm wide and massed 785 grams. *Self-contained missiles* was more like it. Each of them had a tiny, fusion-powered generator and a powered injector system. Firing the round down the barrel of the weapon initiated the generator and armed the injector. When the round hit a Grub's force field, the injector fired, and the rocket assist drove the round into the Grub's body. Once inside, the generator would flare, disrupting the Grub's internal energy production, essentially canceling it out.

Unlike his shielding, these had been through limited testing. Select Marines had used them last month during a fight on some nameless planet, and they had proven to be at least partially effective. A single round would not take out a Grub, but it would piss it off to no end. Four or five rounds could kill one.

The problem with the rounds was that they were wickedly difficult to manufacture, and the 28 rounds in his magazine had cost more than Hondo would ever earn in his lifetime.

To back up his M96, he had a pike (the same kind as he had used against the Grubs before), his Ruger, and an FN P30, a sleek bullpup dart-thrower used by the Confederation Special Forces. The Ruger and the FN wouldn't have any effect against a Grub, but there were more dangers in the universe than them, and Hondo had been warned about wasting one of his M96 rounds against the local equivalent of a guard dog.

It was time. He took a deep breath, focusing on calming himself. He couldn't afford letting his nerves get the better of himself. In every other engagement, he had Marines to his side, Marines he could count on. But this time, it was just him. Ben, waiting to do the snatch, couldn't help.

"Are you in position?" he asked Ben.

He was about to kick it off, so if the Grubs were somehow monitoring his transmissions, there wasn't any reason to keep off the net now.

"Roger, I'm ready," Ben passed back.

Let's do it, McKeever! he thought, jumping up and beginning to run at the nearest Grub, closing the distance.

The big Grub didn't seem to notice him. No pseudopods formed, no light tendrils reached out to envelope him. At 50 meters away, Hondo started to slow down, M96 at the ready. Laser-focused on the Grub, he inadvertently stepped on the purple moss, almost losing his footing. He jumped back, risking a look down. He could swear the moss was aware of him, and it seemed to flow towards his feet.

No time for that. Keep focused.

Hondo stepped around the moss, waiting for some sort of reaction from the Grubs, but it was as if he wasn't even there.

"They're ignoring me," he passed to Ben as he got to 25 meters away. "I'm going to fire. You be ready."

"Roger. I'm ready."

Hondo aimed his M96 as the middle of the Grub. They could change their shape, and no one knew which part was their most vulnerable, but the middle seemed like as good a target as any. Slowing his breathing, he pressed the trigger. A single round whizzed down the barrel, then struck the Grub, the injector detonating in a flash of light.

Hondo couldn't see the round itself activate inside the Grub, but he could see the results. The Grub contracted into a sphere and squealed in agony, only the third time that Hondo had ever heard a Grub make a sound. It quivered, contracting and expanding, waves of low-level blue light sweeping across its body.

Hondo held off firing again, swinging his M96 to cover the other three Grubs, who were more than 100 meters away on the other side of the babies. They had frozen in place, two of them raising part of their bodies as if to get a better view—not that they had discernable eyes of any kind.

The babies were doing nothing. They kept eating the moss, uninterrupted.

Hondo was confused. He'd been ready for action, ready to fight to the death. He hadn't been ready for this. The pulsing waves of light on the Grub he'd shot were slowing down, but that was about it. The other three Grubs weren't doing anything.

"This isn't working. I'm going to hit the other three. As soon as that happens, move in," he told Ben.

The Grub he'd hit wasn't dead. He'd hurt it, but it looked to be handling the damage. If he shot the other three, he'd be out four of his 29 rounds and still have four wounded Grubs to contend with. If they lashed out, he doubted that he'd be able to handle things. If Ben could get in and snatch one of the babies, then they might be able to hightail it back to the podsuits and extract before the Grubs could recover enough to react.

Hondo stood upright, and taking careful aim, fired three rounds, one at each remaining Grub. Two reacted as had the first, contracting into a sphere. The third flattened out and started zigzagging in what looked to be a mindless fashion. The babies never reacted. From the the other side of the Grubs, Ben darted forward into sight, a ziplock in hand.

Ziplocks were the medical stasis bags used to stabilize wounded or dead Marines until they could be taken out of stasis at a medical facility. The scientist-types had determined that the stasis field would work on a baby Grub as well, stopping all cellular activity. They just had to get one of them inside the bag before activating the field.

That was going to be Ben's problem.

Hondo ran forward to a spot on the dirt in the middle of the babies, watching the four Grubs for any sign of offensive action. Ben reached the edge of the babies, then hesitated as if trying to pick one.

"Just get any of them," Hondo shouted.

Ben raised an upper hand in acknowledgment, then carefully stepped onto the moss to reach one of the babies, open ziplock held over it. With the swoop of a diving osprey, he pounced . . . and light exploded, rippling across the moss and lighting up the baby like a torch.

"Ben!" Hondo shouted, rushing to his teammate.

Ben was on his back, off the moss, his four arms upwards, but curled at the elbows, his neck arched back, and neck frill fully displayed. Tiny sparks fell from his frill's feathers. Hondo slid on his knees to a stop beside his teammate, reaching for his lower armpit.

As part of an Interrecon team, he'd learned basic Klethos first aid, but he couldn't handle much more than stuffing Ben in a ziplock if it came to that. To his relief, he felt the rapid, almost vibration-like pulse of the Klethos' blue blood coursing through his body. He was alive.

With a human-like groan, Ben straightened his head, opened his eyes, and looked at Hondo.

"What happened?"

"You got lit up like a Christmas tree, that's what happened."

"Did I get the Grub?" he asked, turning his head to look.

The ziplock was still on the moss in a crumpled mess, smoke wisping up. That was a good sign that the stasis generator was fried. The babies had stopped moving, and the moss had faint waves of light passing through the patch.

Hondo swiveled to look at the big Grubs. They hadn't moved, but the pulsing lights had lessened. The one that had been bounding about had stopped, and it was contracting into to a sphere now as well. To him, that indicated they were recovering from the rounds. He could shoot them again, but he would rather collect the baby Grub and get out of there before that.

But how to snatch a baby? He'd just seen what had happened to Ben, who was only now slowly sitting up. A Klethos was a far sturdier creature than a human was, and he'd have probably been killed by the same discharge of energy that had knocked Ben silly.

The patch of moss in front of them was about 20 meters by 30, and there were probably close to 80 babies on it. None were on the bare dirt that he could see. But ten meters away, one of the babies was right at the edge of the moss.

"Wait here," he told Ben, then stood up and approached the baby.

Standing on the dirt, he could reach out and touch it if he wanted, but he held back. It was motionless. He didn't even know if it was alive, but it didn't seem to be hurt. He reached out with one hand, tempted to just jerk the thing back, but one look over at Ben, who was hunched over, elbows wrapped around his knees, gave him pause.

The lights sweeping through the moss were diminishing, both in frequency and intensity. Hondo wasn't sure how all of this was connected, but there was obviously something going on. The babies were feeding on the moss, somehow, and the moss was full of energy that could be discharged. Either the moss was somehow "charging" the babies directly, or the discharge was a defensive measure. Either way, it could kill him. He didn't know if it had more then one charge, or if not, how long it would take it to recharge on its own, and Hondo was not in the mood to touch it and find out.

He looked down at his M96. He did have a weapon designed to counteract Grub energy.

Before he even thought it out, Hondo lowered the weapon and fired into the middle of the moss. Immediately, the moss illuminated a bright, blinding light. An aura surrounded him for a moment, but whether the cerrostrands deflected it or it was something else, Hondo didn't know.

He dropped his M96 and grabbed the P30 off his back. The P30 had a pistol grip. He reversed it and grabbed the barrel, pushing the butt over the closest Grub. With one quick hook, he pulled back, the pistol grip hitting the far side of the baby Grub. He gave it a strong tug, and the Grub flipped up and over off the moss.

Hondo was working on instinct here. For all he knew, the blast that hit Ben had come from the Grub and not the moss, but there was only one way to find out. He pulled his ziplock from his cargo pocket, opened it, and spread it over the baby Grub, careful not to touch the thing. Shifting to the end, he started sealing it, pulling the far side under the Grub as he did so. With enough jerking and shifting, he managed to pull the material around it and finished closing it off before he hit the stasis button.

He released the breath he hadn't realized he was holding. The stasis started kicking in just as the Grub started to move inside the ziplock. Within a few moments, it stopped moving, and within another minute, the green indicator lit. Stasis was achieved.

I can't believe we did it, he thought, as he bent over and peered inside the clear panel.

"I think we should get out of here," Ben said, stepping up alongside him.

"How are you doing?"

"I've been better, but I'm regaining function."

The first Grub Hondo had shot was beginning to elongate into the more common cigar shape. It was evidently recovering, and Hondo agreed. It was time to diddiho.

Hondo bent down to lift the ziplocked Grub onto his shoulder and grunted with the effort. The baby Grub looked to be about the size of a small person, but it weighed much more, at least

150 kgs, he thought. He settled his feet to get a better lift when Ben stepped up and pushed him aside.

"I've got this," he said. "You cover me."

Hondo wanted to object. He could bench press 150 kg, dead lift 300, but he would be straining. Ben, even after being shocked, didn't have much trouble lifting the baby Klethos by the carrying straps on the ziplock. Macho posturing aside, Ben was the better choice.

"Stay off of the moss," he said as Ben started off.

"You don't have to tell me that," Ben said. "My frill is still standing on end."

Hondo followed Ben across the open area, walking backwards and keeping an eye on the adult Grubs. They hadn't shown any sign of aggression, but with one of their babies missing, Hondo wasn't going to assume it was going to stay that way.

He was missing the boat on that, but his vigilance was warranted. Just as they were approaching the tree line, a light tendril reached out for them, glancing off Hondo's chest, but making every nerve in his body tingle. From beyond the babies and four Grubs, two more Grubs appeared from where Ben had been laying in wait, and there was no doubt that they were locked onto the two Interrecon teammates.

"Run, Ben. I'll hold them off!"

He dropped to a knee, raised his M96, and fired a long 800-meter shot just as another tendril of light reached out from the nearer of the two new Grubs. Hondo dropped to the ground as his round hit, and the Grub's tendril swept crazily across the nearest trees as the Grub reacted violently, smashing into the other newcomer.

"Get back to your podsuit," he passed to Ben. "I'll try to lead them off."

Ben didn't try to protest. He knew that the baby in the ziplock took precedence over either one of them.

Hondo took advantage of the confusion and bolted back to the trees, hoping that they would give him some cover. For all he knew, the trees were also part of the Grubs' ecosystem, just like the moss was. If so, another strike by the two new Grubs would set them all off. His guts told him that they were native, though, and not part of the Grub universe. He hoped they would give him cover. He got behind one of the large trees, then peered around.

The second Grub had passed the first and was heading towards him at top speed while the second seemed to be reorienting itself. The lead Grub fired again, the light slashing against the tree. Bits of light seemed to fall free and sweep around the tree, setting Hondo's nerves alight again, but he didn't think he received a direct hit.

If his Brotherhood shielding did work, he was losing confidence that it would save him from a full blast. He couldn't just sit there and wait for the Grubs to reach him—he had to take the fight to them.

Hondo leaned past the cover of the tree and fired two rounds. At least one of them struck true. The lead Grub barely faltered and kept advancing. It shot another tendril of light that struck the tree trunk a meter over Hondo's head—the trunk cracked, and steam poured up, the heat making Hondo step back just as the top of the tree fell over.

Hondo was already moving, but the fleshy fronds of the falling tree hit him in the back, knocking him to the ground. If he'd bolted a split second later, the heavy bole would have hit him. He scrambled to his feet and fired once more before darting behind another tree.

This time, the Grub slowed to a stop. It slightly contracted, swirls of light revolving around the area just above the round's point of impact. Hondo fired again, but this time, there was no reaction.

The thing's as big as a freaking house, and I missed it? How the hell did I do that?

He looked down at his weapon, checking the readouts. The Grub was at 450 meters, and that was reflected on his M96's display. Hondo had fired over 500 rounds of practice ammo before the mission, and he was fairly confident of his abilities with the weapon, but something had to be wrong.

Hondo had pushed up his monocle to fire his weapon. Unlike a helmet or PICS display, the monocles took getting used to. The brain had to ignore what was being seen by the left eye when a

Marine wanted to see what the monocle over the right eye was displaying and vice-versa when he wanted to see with his left eye. Hondo had mastered the process, but as with most Marines, doing it too long gave him a headache, so the default position for most Marines was with the monocle flipped up.

Hondo flipped the monocle back down, then turned on the scanner. He stood, got a good cheek weld, and fired center mass on the lead Grub. The monocle picked up the trace, enhancing it to a bright red swath . . . and the round went high, just skimming over the top of his target. He ranged the Grub again, but this time with his monocle: 447 meters, the same as his M96 had ranged it.

And it hit him. For all the money spent developing the weapon, the actual round's characteristics were not entered correctly. The practice rounds were fine, but not the real deal.

An armorer could fix this problem, but not Hondo. He had to resort to Kentucky windage. He flipped off the automatic targeting system, found the suggested aiming point, then lowered two meters and fired. This time, the trace led right to the Grub, slightly below his intended point of impact, but a hit nonetheless.

The Grub shuddered, and the swirls of light changed to bolts traversing the thing's body. The trailing Grub, the one Hondo had already hit, came alongside of it, firing a light tendril that reached out for him. It was as if his entire body came alight with an intense itch, and he barely managed to dive out of the light's reach. His cerrostrand shielding was working . . . to a point. He was still alive, but he knew it was only a matter of time until his shielding failed.

From his prone position, he couldn't see into the open area. He got to his knees to see that the trailing Grub was now in the lead, charging across to him, now about 300 meters away. Hondo fired twice more, taking the time to manually aim. Both rounds hit home, and the Grub squalled a piercing screech—whether in pain or anger, Hondo didn't know.

Light tendrils shot out haphazardly towards the trees. Hondo ducked; it would suck to get taken out by an un-aimed spray of light. A splinter from an exploding tree hit him in his back with a hard blow, but his STF armor hardened to keep him from being pierced.

The light show slowed, and Hondo risked taking a peek. One of the Grubs was slowly retreating, a sickly blue light moving from one end of it to the other. The second Grub was still 300 meters out, slowly collapsing like a deflating balloon. Sometimes, Grubs exploded in a last orgy of energy, but this one simply let go.

Hondo stood up to watch. He couldn't believe it. As angry as he was about the aiming program for the combat rounds, he had to admit that the rounds themselves worked as advertised. Three rounds had killed one Grub, and three more had forced one to retreat. If they could manage to get the raw materials and pump more of them out, then humans and Klethos might stand a chance at turning back the Grub tide.

And then the world around Hondo erupted into light and sound: the sound from exploding trees, the light from . . . it had to be more Grubs. Hondo was blown to the ground again, a lance of pain jabbing his knee as his leg hit awkwardly. As he lay stunned, an intense light tendril swept through the trees over his head, mowing the tops like wheat before the scythe. Unlike wheat, though, the trees were exploding in splinters and steam. Hondo scrambled on his back to get out of the impact area, just missing getting crushed by falling tree-tops twice.

"Ben, what's your status? I'm getting the shit pummeled out of me here."

"I'm four klicks from my podsuit. I'll let you know when I've activated it."

Hondo couldn't see who was firing at him, but he knew it had to be at least two more Grubs. It could be the other four nanny-types, but something told him that it had to be new ones in the warrior mold. It had to be at least two because the tendril slashing through the forest was one of the enhanced ones, the ones that the Grubs converged to take down atmospheric planes and even spaceships. If one of those tendrils even touched him, then no simple suit shielding would protect him.

And a simple touch would shoot down a Klethos escaping in a podsuit.

Hondo wanted to run as fast as his legs would carry him, run to his podsuit and get off the planet, but Ben had to escape. Hondo had to cover him—no, not just cover him. He had to take out the threat.

Hondo had now personally killed three Grubs in his career, three-point-five if he got credit for the assist on K1003. If he were a sniper with their propensity for tallies, he'd have the second-highest Grub kill number in the Marine Corps, and third overall, trailing Gunny Hatori and the Confederation's Specialist Six Nianci. He'd managed that by being in the right place at the right time (or, as some would argue, in the wrong place at the wrong time) and with a huge helping of luck. There were at least two more Grubs out there that he had to stop, and he was pretty sure his luck well had just about run dry.

Well, it's been a good run.

"Ben, listen to me. We've got at least two more Grubs here, and they're merging their tendrils. You can't take off until I give you the OK, understand?"

There was silence on the other end of the comms, then, "At least two? That is a pretty tall order, Hondo. What if you're not around to give me that order?"

As in, if I'm already dead?

"Monitor my vitals," he said. "Keep your monocle in place."

If anything, the Klethos had more problems with the monocles than the Marines did, and they had a tendency to ignore them, just as the females had a tendency to ignore the full helmet displays.

"If I go down, take off immediately before they can reorient. Keep low and try to get to the other side of the planet before taking off."

The podsuits were simple transports in reality, able to cross the black, but they were not particularly maneuverable in an atmosphere. Still, that seemed like the best course of action to him.

"Understand. I will comply," Ben passed. A moment later, he added, "Semper fi, Marine."

Hondo felt a warm wave come over him. Ben was not a Marine. Only eight of those in Interrecon were Federation Marines, in fact. But brotherhood was brotherhood, something all warriors understood.

"Semper fi, Ben," he passed before cutting his transmission.

Above him, the continuous band of light had switched to bursts, searching the trees for him. The Grubs' Achilles heel was energy expenditure. If they could be induced into indiscriminate fire, then they could be depleted to the point that humans or Klethos could defeat them.

Still, Hondo didn't understand why they just didn't lower their point of aim and root him out on the ground. He wasn't complaining, but why aim two or three meters above ground level? That might work for a Klethos female or a Marine in a PICS, but it was off-target to a ground-pounding grunt.

Oh, that's it, he realized. *They don't understand what they're facing.*

He was sure he was right, but he wasn't sure just how he could take advantage of it. An elephant rifle was not the best weapon to take out a mouse, but the bottom line was that a mouse was still a mouse—and *this* mouse had to figure out what to do.

The first thing he had to do was to get out of the line of fire, and knowing the Grubs were aiming high gave him an opening. He got to his knees first, then started to move to his right in a crouch, never lifting his head above a meter-and-a-half. The Grubs kept peppering the trees above him, but gradually, he put a little distance between himself and the danger area. When he was sure that he was out of the immediate line of fire, he cautiously moved forward, using a huge tree trunk as cover. He edged around it, and spotted three Grubs slowly moving across the open area. Every ten seconds or so, they merged a tendril that shot forward.

Hondo checked his load. He'd fired 15 of the rounds, giving him 14 remaining. If it took three rounds per Grub to kill it or make it retreat, then he had a mathematical chance of success—if the Grubs just stood still and let him shoot them. The problem was that enemy fighters had a habit of making things a little more difficult than that.

There was a flash of movement to the right, a large white something just within Hondo's peripheral vision. Reacting on instinct, Hondo wheeled and fired, sending a round into the Grub. It squealed and contracted into a sphere, and Hondo realized his mistake. He'd come around far enough that he'd just fired at one of the original nanny Grubs. Now, he was down another round.

More importantly, he had caught the attention of the three fighters. He could almost see them realizing where he was and starting to swing towards his position. Hondo bolted to the rear, trying to get as many trees between himself and the Grubs as possible when the world erupted into violence behind him. He felt the tiniest of disruptions, just a touch of their blast, but the trees protected him for the moment.

The trees were going down, though, so he turned to his right, back the way he'd come, and ran for all he was worth.

I can't run forever, he knew, forcing himself to slow down and move back to the edge of the trees.

The three Grubs had stopped, two of them firing, but the third one sitting quietly to the side. Hondo was sure that it was using the other two to flush him out, waiting for him to make a mistake, and then it would pounce.

Hondo ranged that Grub, and immediately he saw a reaction. It had detected the laser rangefinder striking it, but he wasn't sure if it could tell exactly from where it had come. Hondo wasn't going to give it the time to figure that out.

At 236 meters, the thing was huge, too big to miss, but Hondo still aimed low and fired. The round hit true, but he shifted his aim before he could see the effect of it and fired on the other two, missing the last one and having to fire again.

A light tendril shot out from the first one, grazing his side. His left arm went numb as he dove back into the cover of the massive trunk.

Holy shit! he thought, as he tried to lift his arm to look.

He'd taken a glancing blow, and his arm was slow to respond. His hand had no feeling at all, and he had no control over it. It was a limp lump of meat, nothing more.

He wasn't in a PICS with its full array of medical capabilities, but his AI was sophisticated enough to inject him with anti-shock nanites. He knew his hand was gone, and he regretted it, but was able to push that to the side. He tested his arm, and it was not much better, but he had minimal control, at least.

The stock of his M96 had also been hit, but there wasn't much in the stock that could be damaged. Hondo checked the weapon, and it was still combat-ready.

He had eight rounds left and three very angry Grubs out there looking to kill him.

It didn't bother him. He knew that was the nanites talking, and he knew that complacency was dangerous, but it was better than being paralyzed from shock.

Hondo tucked the stock of his weapon between his right elbow and his side and stepped around the tree trunk. The three Grubs had split up, each advancing on its own to the trees. He fired three more rounds, two of them hitting the middle Grub and stopping it in its tracks. That was the third hit it had taken, and as with the previous two, that seemed to be the magic number. Hondo put it out of his mind and tried to target the other two as they raced for the trees. He fired at one and missed, his one-handed position handicapping his aim. It started elongating, turning into a huge, snake-like form just as it reached the first trees, and Hondo snapped off two more shots, somehow hitting the trailing end of it just as it entered the forest.

There was an eruption of light, then an explosion, the shock wave almost knocking Hondo to the ground as pseudo-leaves rained down around him.

That's five-point-five of you mother fuckers, he thought, his warrior pride overcoming the nanites.

He ordered his AI to release counter-nanites. He'd accepted the loss of his hand, so he hoped the shock would be subsiding, but he'd couldn't afford the *laissez faire* attitude they'd forced upon him. He'd probably wasted two rounds because of that. Within a minute, he started feeling like Hondo again.

One Grub, three rounds, he thought, looking at his weapon display.

He tried to remember if he'd hit the remaining Grub once or twice. He thought it was only once. That meant he had to hit it twice more with three rounds.

Don't miss.

The Grub was in the trees with him. Hondo was tempted to just bolt. The Grub was huge, even if it had elongated into the same snake-like shape as the other one had. Hondo had to have the advantage there, and even wounded, he thought he could beat the thing back to his podsuit. But even one Grub would be a danger to Ben. The Klethos podsuits were fantastic pieces of technology, but they were very vulnerable to the Grubs' light weapons. No, Hondo had to find it and kill it.

He caught a tiny glimpse of movement through the trees, and he pulled up his M96, but held his fire. It wasn't a clear shot, and he had to make sure that his rounds hit home. But now he knew where it was, so he started his stalk forward.

His hand started to ache something fierce, but he ignored that, straining his senses. The Grub was huge; certainly it would have to make noise as it moved. It was hard enough for Hondo to move silently in the forest detritus.

From his left, light lanced out, glancing off tree trunks as it tried to nail him. His left arm bloomed in fire and Hondo dove to his right. Whereas last time, the hand had gone numb, now he cried out in pain as he landed on the ground.

While I was stalking it, the bastard was stalking me!

He looked at his arm. He wasn't sure if he'd actually been hit—it had looked like the tendril had bounced off the tree ahead and just missed him, but his arm was in agony.

"No painkillers," he ordered his AI.

He had to have his wits about him if he was going to survive this.

The Grub had somehow moved to his left. He lay prone on the ground, peering in that direction, trying to spot it. There was the tiniest bit of movement, and Hondo raised his M96, but once again, he held his fire. He had to be sure.

And then he saw it. Instead of the pasty white color that every other Grub he'd seen had been, it had changed to the same blue-green of the trees' foliage. This had never been reported, to the best of his knowledge. He snapped an image and sent it off to the command as he slowly raised his M96. He didn't have much of a window between the trees, maybe ten centimeters. He already knew that his targeting system wasn't accurate, but that was with regards to range. The Grub was slowly moving across 60 meters to his front, and he thought he could slip the round between the trees.

He tried to aim his M96, but with only his right arm, the barrel wavered ever so slightly. That might be enough to throw off his shot. He swung his legs around and edged up into the sitting position, resting the barrel of the M96 across his knee. Taking up a good sight picture, he pressed the trigger button.

The round ran true, bisecting the space between the trees and slamming into the Grub. The green skin turned back to white as it disappeared from sight with a crashing of the brush.

One more, and two rounds to do it!

For the first time since the warrior Grubs appeared, Hondo began to let himself feel the slightest bit of hope that he might get out of this alive. He backed up against the tree trunk, waiting for the Grub to come to him. It had proven itself to be a better stalker than he was, so let it make a fatal mistake and not him.

For twenty minutes, the forest was silent with no sign of the Grub. A lone orange native animal hesitantly made an appearance on the next tree over, slowly creeping down the tree, scanning the forest for whatever had been invading its little domain. It never saw Hondo sitting silently below it.

And then, finally, Hondo saw the Grub—or part of it. He couldn't even tell how far away it was, but there was no mistaking it. Hondo shifted the aim of his weapon, using his knee as a support.

This is it.

He pressed the trigger and fired, but the round hit the one exposed branch between the Grub and him, detonating the injector early. There was a flash of light as the generator kicked off.

"Shit!" Hondo said, as the orange animal scurried back up the tree and he tried to reacquire the Grub.

It was no longer in his weapon's sight picture, and he flipped up his monocle, sending all his senses forward. He needn't have bothered—there was no way that he could miss the crashing sound as the Grub charged, no way he could miss the light tendrils springing out in all directions.

Hondo held steady. This was his last round, and he had to shoot true. With it coming right at him in the snake-configuration, the aspect was smaller than normal. That gave him a relatively smaller target. He had to wait long enough to ensure a hit, but he also had to shoot it before the tendrils snapping off its body were directed at him.

All those thoughts registered in the few seconds that it took the Grub to close the distance. Hondo touched the trigger just as a light tendril shot out to him. His round hit first, and the finger of flowing Grub-energy shifted to his right as the thing veered away, bouncing off a tree trunk, then careening into another before coming to a stop.

Hondo scrambled to get behind the tree he'd been leaning on, afraid that the Grub was going to blow. When that didn't happen, he leaned around it, his lungs bellowing as adrenaline coursed through his body. The Grub had contracted not into a sphere, but more like the normal torpedo shape. Lights were rotating under its skin, but without the frenetic patterns he'd seen on the others. After a moment, the Grub moved forward a few meters, then stopped again. Without a doubt, the thing was alive, and it seemed to be gathering itself.

Damn you! Don't you know three rounds are supposed to take you out?

Hondo checked his load, already knowing he was at zero. There wasn't an extra round hiding unbeknownst to him. He dropped the 96. It was useless without any ammo, and while the rounds were prohibitively expensive, the weapon itself was no more expensive than a grunt's M99.

He unslung his P30. The carbine shouldn't be able to damage the Grub, but maybe in its damaged state?

He fired a burst of 20 rounds. Nothing. Nada. The Grub didn't even flinch.

"Ben, go now. There's one left, but it's temporarily incapacitated. I think its recovering, though."

"Are there any more around?" Ben asked.

Hondo turned and looked back in the direction of the babies and nannies. He hadn't even considered it, but it would make sense that there were more than five of the fighters on the entire planet.

"I frankly don't know. But I'm out of rounds, so if there are any more, we're shit out of luck. Just make a break for it now."

"Roger, understood. I've got the baby locked in, and I'll be off in 20 seconds."

"Fair winds and following seas, my friend," Hondo said as he counted down the time.

At fifteen seconds, Ben came back on the net with, "You'd better be following me, you human son-of-a-bitch, you."

Hondo couldn't see nor hear Ben take off, but his net noted it as Hondo laughed out loud. Hondo didn't know if Klethos ever swore, or if it was even within their concept. They were all honor this and honor that, and they could be very formalized in their manner of speaking Standard, so the shock of Ben calling him a son-of-a-bitch had caught him off-guard.

"Make it back, Ben," he whispered, before turning his attention to the Grub laying not 20 meters from him.

It had plumped up, for lack of a better term, and the light show under its skin was settling down. Hondo knew it was about to be back into fighting trim. He didn't know how much of its energy reserves remained, but if it had any at all, it was probably more than enough to take a wounded human out. He started to go around it, to try and race back to his podsuit, but his legs were shaking, and if it did recover, it would track him down before he even got halfway there.

He had to end it now.

He had one more weapon that could work. Reaching back with his right hand, he grabbed the neck of his pike and pulled it free. He extended the shaft and checked the power, suddenly afraid that one of the hits or near misses had grounded the charge, but the power LED was a steady green.

A pike was designed to be used with two hands, but Hondo only had one. He tried to position it like an old-time mounted knight with a jousting lance. It didn't feel secure, but it would have to do.

Ahead of him, the Grub started to stir, pseudo-arms appearing and contracting, as if it was testing itself. It swung around to orient itself on Hondo, one of the light-shooting polyps growing and twisting towards him when with a shout, Hondo broke into a run.

The Grub raised up its forequarters as the light-shooting polyp completely emerged. A spark of light appeared at the tip just as Hondo rammed the pike home with all of his weight behind it. He kept driving it for a moment as the Grub started back, trying to push it deeper, waiting for the discharge before he remembered he had to let go. A Marine in a PICS could handle the discharge, but an unprotected Marine would be killed, so it wouldn't activate until he released it.

He jumped back, falling on his ass as he scrambled farther away, his heels and right hand churning on the forest floor.

The Grub froze, its forequarters raised, and Hondo wondered if, after all that, the pike had malfunctioned. Then slowly, ponderously, like a 2D clip he'd once seen of an old-time dirigible, the *Hindenburg,* it slowly collapsed onto the ground, parts of its skin sloughing off as it flattened onto the ground, its leading edge a mere meter from his feet.

Hondo sat there for a moment, watching the remains of the Grub for any sign of movement, any sign of life. There were none. He slowly—and painfully—got to his feet, and with one more look at the Grub's body, gave it a wide berth as he started back to his podsuit.

EARTH

Chapter 2
Skylar

Minister-at-Large Skylar Ybarra stared at the highly classified message. It was only a few short words, but it represented so much more.

Mission on G8 successful. Package is incoming.

She couldn't believe it, and the scientist in her was excited. To think, that after seven years of war, humankind finally had a live Dictymorph to examine. It was reportedly a juvenile, but the wealth of information they could glean from it could very well be the turning point in the fight.

There had been a contingency plan in place for just such an opportunity, and Sky had put things in motion once she'd been told that one of the new Interrecon teams had spotted the Dictymorph young. She'd refused to follow what was happening on the other side of the galaxy, afraid she'd jinx it. She might have two Ph.Ds, she might be the Minister-at-Large to the Federation and Special Advisor for Alien Affairs to the UAM secretary-general, but she still held to some silly superstitions.

Well, it worked. They got it, she told herself, fully aware of the incongruity that represented, of her, a scientist giving superstition any credence.

"Keyshon, what's the status with the mother superior?" she asked her long-time executive assistant over her PA.

"She left Destiny an hour ago, along with her staff. I'll let you know when she arrives, ma'am."

Sky had mad respect for the mother superior, the head of the Saint Peter Canisius Monastery, the Jesuit institution that had become a hub of Dictymorph research. The secret station located deep within the Pak-Sokolov Belt, already had a standing staff ready to spring into action, but the monastery staff had a proven track record, and Sky wanted them to be part of the team. She would have put the mother superior in charge if she thought she could swing it from a political standpoint, but the ill will that had arisen between the Jesuits and the Brotherhood over the Brotherhood's aborted withdrawal from the war effort made that impractical. In her new dual-hatted position, she could have forced the issue, but she was beginning to understand the political aspect of her job. She hadn't needed Keyshon to remind her that such a move could cause friction in the still-rocky alliance.

The Jesuits didn't need to be in charge, anyway. As long as they had access, they could contribute.

Sky tapped the ship icon on the top bar of her PA, pulling up the status of her ship. All systems were go. She could catch a hover to the spaceport and be on her way to the secret station in 45 minutes. She ached to do it. She was a scientist, damn it, not a bureaucrat.

She knew that wasn't true, though, as much as she hated to admit it. She had initially gained the notice of the Federation's Second Minister based on her academic study of the Klethos, but each promotion had taken her further away from research and deeper into the bureaucracy. Convincing the Brotherhood to come back into the fold, and thereby averting a Klethos attack on them had cemented her place within the government, first as the newly created Minister-at-Large for the Federation, and then as the Special Advisor to the UAM's secretary-general.

Still, I've got the power. I've got the ship at my beck and call. Who's to say that overseeing the research on the juvenile Dictymorph isn't where I should be?

As if overhearing her thoughts, her EPA vibrated. She pulled it out of her pocket, knowing who would be on the other line. Fewer than twenty people had access to the high-level, secure net. If she had really thought that she could just slip away, then the call disabused her of that fanciful notion.

She thumbed open the line and said, "Chairman Hrbec, you are probably calling about our newest acquisition. Let me tell you where we are now . . ."

No, her place was here in Brussels. This is what she'd become.

GOLDEN HAPPINESS STATION

Chapter 3
Hondo

Hondo stepped off the *FSS Vargas Voyager* and into the clean, almost antiseptic smell of *Golden Happiness Station*. Usually, stations were a miasma of odors that the scrubbers were never able to remove, but as a brand-new—and highly classified--station, it had that just-from-the-package smell. This was the first, and probably last time, he'd ever experience that in a station anywhere.

A Navy captain (the equivalent of a Marine full bird colonel) was waiting for them at the hatch. He stepped up as the two Interrecon teammates appeared, seemingly anxious to coral them.

"Staff Sergeant McKeever, Team Member Ben, if you would both follow me?" he asked, although it wasn't really a question.

"Just a second, sir, if you'll allow it," Hondo said, surprising himself by interrupting someone of the captain's rank.

Behind them, a team of sailors was guiding a large, enclosed mule out of the hatch and into the station. Six armed civilian guards—whose manner bespoke of years in the service—met them, and together, they moved the mule down the snake tube and into the station proper.

"Sorry, sir, but I just wanted to watch our—" the captain interrupted him by holding up his palm.

"Your *package* has arrived safe and sound, Staff Sergeant. Now, if you would follow me?"

"*Package*," Ben chortled behind Hondo.

With the female Klethos, Hondo had never observed what he'd thought was a sense of humor, but the longer he was around Ben, the more he was convinced that he looked at the universe differently and found much of what he saw amusing. Hondo wasn't sure if that was particular only to Ben, particular to all male Klethos, or just to any Klethos who was not a warrior.

Hondo gave Ben a slight come-along gesture with his good right hand, then followed the captain down several corridors, then into a compartment.

He couldn't help but notice the red lights around the hatch, a sure sign that this was a secured compartment and proof against any type of covert surveillance.

I thought we were all friends here, he thought wryly.

Waiting in the compartment was a middle-aged civilian man and a Marine major. The two stood up as they entered and proffered their hands to be shaken. Hondo complied, noting with surprise that the civilian's handshake was firm, more so than the major's. Ben, used to the ways of humans, took both of their hands at the same time, the civilian getting his upper right and the major the lower right. Hondo thought he saw the tiniest of glints in the Klethos' eye.

Is he having fun with this?

The civilian, Deputy Director of Blah-Blah-Blah Hansen (Hondo didn't catch exactly what he was deputy director of, but from the man's tone, he seemed to think he was pretty important, at least), had little time for civil formalities. He thanked them for their service, told them they were going to undergo several days of debriefing by the station staff, and to be . . . not dishonest, not reticent, but *careful* of what they offered. Anything that could be controversial needed to be cleared with either him or the Navy captain before they mentioned it.

Controversial? We're frigging grunts. We fought some Grubs. What could be controversial about that?

Hondo looked over at Ben, but he couldn't discern any sort of reaction. Interrecon was under the command of the UAM task force, not the Federation. Hondo was a Marine, and he was answerable to the Corps and Federation, but Ben was a Klethos. Yet, here was some Federation bureaucrat giving him orders? The male Klethos were not as honor-bound as the females, but this might be pushing things a little too far.

The civilian went on for 20 minutes. Hondo listened with one ear. Unless the major or even the captain gave him a direct order to withhold information, and maybe even not then, he was going to be forthright with what he knew. When he accepted orders to Interrecon, he'd essentially given his loyalty for the duration.

"And finally, once you leave this station, you will not be authorized to tell anyone what has transpired. Not your wife, not your kids, not your parents, not anyone. Understand?"

This guy doesn't know anything about me, Hondo thought. *He never asked for a brief. And he can't be serious with Ben.*

Hondo wasn't married, didn't have kids. The Klethos didn't even have the concept of marriage.

"Yes, sir," Hondo said, trying to keep the frown off his face.

He already knew that his missions were highly classified, and that everything that he saw or did was to remain a secret, so he didn't have a problem with the order. He just thought the man could have taken twenty seconds to pull up his personal information.

The man looked pleased with himself as he stood, shook hands once more, and left the compartment, trailed by the captain.

"Staff Sergeant McKeever, Team Member Ben, I'm Major John Worthington. I'm a Marine liaison to the station, and I'm your minder while you are here," he said, shrugging as he said the word "minder."

"Team Member Ben, for you, this is only a courtesy, one you can refuse. But we don't have any Klethos permanently on the station."

"I would be most grateful if you will be my minder," Ben said.

Hondo tried to detect a note of sarcasm in Ben's voice, and once again, he was reminded that while he considered Ben a friend, he was still an alien being, not a human. He couldn't read into things with Ben as he could with a fellow Marine.

"I would be honored, Team Member Ben."

"Just Ben is fine, Major."

"Team Member" was the default title given to the Klethos in Interrecon as if it was impossible to be in the military without a rank that codified a position within the hierarchy. The Klethos did not have rank equivalents, but they put up with the human need for them.

The major nodded, then looked at Hondo, saying, "I'm afraid that the task force command is waiting for their initial shot at you, so we can't take you to sickbay yet. But I promise that once the initial brief is over, I'll run interference for you, and we'll get you seen."

Hondo glanced at his left hand, encased in a stasis sleeve. The *FSS Vargas Voyager*, the Navy surveillance ship disguised as a commercial freighter, did not have a Class A sickbay, and the independent corpsmen onboard couldn't do much more for his hand than slip on the sleeve. Hondo needed a fully-equipped hospital to start the regeneration process.

"It's been this long already, sir. A little later won't hurt anything."

"Still, we don't make it a habit of ignoring a Marine's personal health, even under the circumstances. I may be your minder, but that also means I'm here for you."

"So, you won't let them dissect my brain to see what I might have forgotten, sir?" Hondo asked in jest to move away from the topic.

"You'd be surprised, Staff Sergeant, by what might have been discussed."

What?

Hondo had been joking, and now he couldn't tell if the major was. He'd come close to getting a "harmless" memory mine before, and he didn't want anyone poking around his brain.

"Well, they've got a committee salivating to talk to you now, so let's get this show on the road," the major said, opening the hatch.

Hondo followed the Marine out, hoping against hope that they'd leave their fingers out of his mind.

Chapter 4
Hondo

"I can authorize the transfer to take place as soon as you're done here," Dr. Josief-Anderson said. "We can start right away with the regen."

Hondo hadn't made it to sickbay—the station's "medical facility," seeing as it was under civilian control—for three full days. Every minute he wasn't eating, shitting, or getting in his few brief snatches of shut-eye, had been taken up by debriefs upon debriefs.

He frankly didn't know what else he could tell him, and this after the first 20 minutes. He and Ben had snatched the baby Grub, that was it. It was up to the eggheads to figure out what made them tick. He was just the GalEx delivery man, not the expert on what was in the package.

Every microsecond of his recordings on the planet had been dissected, patched back together, and dissected again, each time with a second-by-second commentary extracted from him. Sometimes he and Ben were being debriefed together, sometimes separately. Ben seemed to be taking all of this in stride and with the patience of a saint, but Hondo was past getting over it. He just wanted to leave.

And now this civilian doctor seemed almost to be offering him an out. He could go back to any Class A hospital, which would include Holcomb Station as one of the possibilities. Cara Riordan had already been transferred off Aegis 2 and on to her next duty station on Tarawa, but Lauren was still at Holcomb and would be for another four months. Hondo wasn't sure if he and Lauren were officially a thing—a love life was very difficult to achieve when two people were in the service and with orders to different duty stations—but he liked her company, and going through regen on Holcomb would at least give them four months together.

"And how long did you say regen would take, sir?" he asked the doctor.

"Well, as I told you, your hand is a total loss. It would have to come off before the regen process can start. And hands are difficult, as you know. An entire arm or just the hand, they surprisingly take about the same amount of time. Every case is different, but I would guess it would take somewhere in the fifteen to eighteen-month time frame."

"Eighteen months? That's a long time to be out of the front lines," Hondo said, more to himself than to the doctor.

"Yes, eighteen months of a regular schedule, with time to yourself. Your job would be to heal, not go chasing Dictymorphs across the galaxy."

Hondo looked up at the man in surprise. Staying off the front lines was a bad thing, not a good thing. He didn't want to skate into some do-nothing, out-of-the-way billet while his fellow Marines put their lives on the line. This guy, this *civilian*, thought he was doing Hondo a favor.

He fought to keep from saying something stupid—the man may be a civilian, but this was a civilian station, and he certainly out-ranked a simple Marine staff sergeant. Hondo didn't need anyone to have him in his crosshairs.

"Thank you, sir, and I appreciate the offer. But you did say something about a prosthetic?"

"Well, yes, we can do that, but no matter how good modern prosthetics are, they can't match your organic arm."

That's not what I heard. They're stronger, can do more, and after learning how to use them, they're even more sensitive to touch.

Hondo didn't say that, however. There were more than a few Marines on active duty with prosthetics. His second battalion commander had two prosthetic legs, and the guy could run half of the Marines in the battalion into the dirt. For him, it made sense, though, because he'd have lost his command as soon as he started regen, and no Marine officer would willingly give up a command.

Then there was Gunny de Nero at Camp Charles, with his shiny, metallic-coated hand. Prosthetic hands could be made to mimic organic hands, but the scuttlebutt was that the Gunny kept his shiny and bright to remind the recruits what the risks were as a Marine.

"Sir, I appreciate your concern, and I can see you've got my best interests at heart, but I think for now, maybe it would be best to get a prosthetic."

The doctor looked surprised, and then said, "Son, you do know that Boosted Regenerative Cancer is a thing of the past, right? We can control it for the rest of your life."

Now it was Hondo's turn to be surprised. He'd thought the Brick was an old-time disease. Back in the old Corps, maybe 20% of those who had regen two or more times came down with it, but he thought it had been eradicated. From what the doctor was saying, it wasn't gone, just controlled.

If Hondo had already been leaning towards a prosthetic, this pushed him even more in that direction.

"Uh . . . yes, sir. I know that. But it's just that . . . well . . . I'm part of Interrecon, one of only eight . . . seven Federation Marines who are part of it. I've got to get back to my unit."

"Get back, only to go out again? I don't know if you realize it, Sergeant, but you're lucky to be alive.

"Staff Sergeant," not "Sergeant" he thought sourly.

"Not everyone will make it back."

Which was true. *Törzsőrmester* Horace Lakatos and Team Member Victor had also spotted Grub babies, but they hadn't survived the snatch attempt. Four other teams—one of them with a fellow Marine—had been killed. Out of 24 teams, 19 were still alive and functioning. He hoped it wasn't hubris speaking, but he and Ben were too valuable to the war for him to simply check out for 18 months.

"I understand that, sir, but it's my duty."

"Your duty is to get killed?"

What the hell are you doing on the Golden Toilet if you aren't dedicated to the cause, Doc?

Hondo took a deep, measured breath, then said, "Sir, as I understand it, this is my decision, and I want a prosthetic. Can you do that here?"

Hondo could see the disgust sweep across the doctor's face, but the man shrugged and said, "Yes, I can. We can have your hand off tomorrow, fit you for a prosthetic, and have a placeholder on by Wednesday. Two days of biofeedback refining, and you'll have the basic capabilities. Once you get back to a major facility, you can get something a little more personalized.

"I still think you're being foolish. You've done your job, you've made your sacrifices, but no one is that vital to the war effort. Not even a Marine. But it's your call. I can schedule you for 1600 this afternoon."

Hondo didn't hesitate, but said, "Let's do it."

The doctor turned to the nurse who'd been standing silently throughout the conversation and said, "Ferdinand, get surgery locked on. And get a four-fifteen ready for the sergeant's signature and scan. You can go over the legalese with him."

Hondo figured the "415" had to be some sort of release. He was going to lose his real hand, after all, and they would want proof that this was his choice.

He looked down at it for a moment, twisting his arm and looking at the hand. He'd taken it for granted all his life. That hand had blown bubbles and played with his X-Fighter model as a kid, had helped play game after game of Dragonlord, had felt Anenyasha Manyika's breast in back of the school one wonderful day, and had caught the bushball saving a try and keeping the provincial championship with his high school. This was the hand that had killed, too, both human and Grub. It had taken lives.

And now, it was just a piece of meat. Dead meat.

"Are you having second thoughts?" the doctor asked hopefully.

Fuck it. It's not doing me any good now, and I can always regen later.

"No, sir. With all due respect, just take this damned thing off and give me something better."

Chapter 5

Skylar

"Welcome, Vice-Minister Ybarra," a familiar voice said, as Sky stepped through the gate and into the terminal, followed by the ever-present Keyshon.

"Reverend Mother, it is so good to see you," Sky said, her face breaking out into a smile. "And please, call me Sky."

The trip to *Golden Happiness Station* had been fraught with work, but the underlying reason for her visit had been gnawing at her the entire time. It was good to see her friend before she had to deal with her fellow bureaucrats, people who were not happy with her coming, afraid that she was poaching on their little slices of the pie.

Sky had no interest in assuming any more bureaucratic headaches, so the others were safe in their little fiefdoms. She wished she was back on Earth, all things considered—not that she hadn't been curious to see what was going on at the station, but rather for the circumstances that brought her here.

"Good to see you too, dear, and please, 'mother superior' is just my day job. Call me Sister Keiko, if you don't mind."

That surprised Sky. She wasn't up on the proper addresses for nuns, monks, and the like, and she'd thought "mother superior" or "reverend mother" were correct. But if the woman wanted to be called Sister Keiko, that was fine with her.

"I hope I was not being too presumptuous, but I thought I might throw a little dozer for you instead of letting the 'crats mob you."

For the second time in ten seconds, Sky looked at the mother superior in surprise. For some reason, she hadn't considered that the woman would even know the positions played in etherball, where a dozer cleared the way for the chucker to go in for a score, and she didn't think the woman would use the somewhat derogatory term "crats."

Still, she was grateful for the woman running interference for her. If the two suits hovering nearby with anxious looks on their faces were any indication, then she would have been mobbed without the woman there. She'd seen it enough back on Earth. Whenever a bigwig appeared, the locals would put on a "dog-and-pony show," as the Marines and Navy called them, scripted performances that kept the worthy from seeing the ground truth and asking tough questions.

Sky had no interest, though, in the running of the station. She was here to get some answers about the research, pure and simple, and she wanted to talk to the scientists face-to-face.

The mother superior led her down the terminal passage to the entrance into the station proper where security stopped her. They knew who Sky was, of course, and they treated her with deference, but this was a Class 1 secured installation, and even she had to be screened. Sky always hated the subsonic scan, which she swore made her bones vibrate, but the rest of the checks were pretty innocuous.

"If you don't mind, Sky, I'd like for you to meet someone before we reach the lab spaces," the mother superior said, after making it past security and into the main corridor on the A level.

"Mother . . . Sister Keiko, I appreciate you meeting me, but I've got limited time here. I'd rather get right to the labs."

"This will only take a minute, but I think you'll appreciate it." She stopped, eyebrows raised in question. "He's right there," she added, pointing at a hatch ten meters down a cross corridor.

Sky didn't want to take the time. She wasn't lying about how little time she had on the station. Both the Federation chairman and the UAM secretary-general were waiting for her personal observations to weigh against the formal reports that had been forwarded up the different chains of command. Still, the woman looked eager, and a couple of minutes more wouldn't make much of a difference.

She hesitated for only a moment, then nodded, stepping up and through the open hatch. She immediately recognized the tall Marine standing there.

"Staff Sergeant McKeever, it's good to see you!" she blurted out, automatically coming in for a hug that she shifted to a handshake at the last moment.

She'd been more than surprised to read in the report that it was the staff sergeant and his Klethos teammate who'd managed to snatch the Dictymorph sample. For all of the now million or so Marines in the expanded, war-footing Corps, she kept crossing paths with this particular Marine, and she probably wouldn't be alive today if it were not for him. This was the fourth time they'd met, and only the first time that hadn't involved combat.

"It's good to meet you again, ma'am."

"And this time, you aren't saving me, Staff Sergeant," she said with a huge smile plastered over her face.

She looked at his left hand, which had an odd-looking Marine camouflage pattern.

"I read that you were injured," she said, nodding at the hand in concern.

He raised the hand and rotated it, then said, "Lost that one. The Grub . . . uh, Dictymorph, tried to ghost me, but all he ghosted was the hand."

"That's an unusual prosthetic, Staff Sergeant. Is regen a problem?"

She hadn't heard that injuries suffered at the hands of the Dictymorphs presented regeneration issues, but there weren't that many who were injured and not irrevocably killed, so it was possible the sample was not large enough to determine trends like that.

"No, ma'am. I just didn't want to take a year-and-a-half to get back up to fighting trim. I've got a feeling that we're going to need every swinging di—" he started to say, before grimacing and looking at the two women. "I mean, we're going to need every single person if we're going to win."

Sky gave a quick glance at the mother superior. If she knew what the Marine had been about to say, she didn't let on, nor did she seem shocked in the least.

"The camouflage is interesting," she said.

"I knew a gunny who kept his a shiny silver, so I figured what the heck. It's not like I need a social hand."

Typical Marine, she thought, holding back a smile.

As she'd met more and more Marines, they'd taken over a soft spot in her heart. With those kind of men and women, she felt more confident that they could prevail—if the science-types could give them the tools they needed.

"Well, I'm about to get briefed on the latest findings. Will you be there, too?"

A cloud seemed to pass over the Marine's face, and the mother superior laughed and said, "I'm afraid the sergeant has been grilled to the gills, and I don't think he wants to have any more to do with those of us in science."

"He's a *staff* sergeant, Reverend Mother, not a sergeant," Sky said almost automatically.

The mother superior looked confused, and she asked, "That's a sergeant, right? What did I say?"

McKeever looked uncomfortable, but Sky was familiar by now with more Marine traditions that she had known existed. Marines could be sticklers for traditions, and calling a staff sergeant, gunnery sergeant, or any of the higher enlisted ranks a "sergeant"was tantamount to "cutting off their heads and pissing in their skulls," as one grizzled colonel had crudely put it.

"Only sergeants, E5's, should be called sergeants. All the higher forms should be addressed with their full rank, except for gunnery sergeants and master sergeants. Gunnery sergeants can be 'gunny' and master sergeants 'top.' But none are ever just 'sergeant.'"

The mother superior still looked confused, and she turned to the staff sergeant and asked, "Is that true, son?"

"Well, yes, Reverend Mother. The ma'am is right."

"Then why have you never mentioned that to me before?"

The Marine squirmed, clearly uncomfortable, but he said, "Because you're a . . . uh . . ."

"Posh, *Staff Sergeant*. Jesuits are not uncivilized ascetics, living as hermits in caves. We're still part of society, and we do know how to mind our P's and Q's. You could have told me."

There was an awkward pause, and Sky broke it with, "Well, it was good to see you again. I've got limited time here on the station, but if I've got time, and if you are free, I'd love to touch base with you before I leave. You and your Klethos partner."

"Sure, ma'am. I mean, I'm just waiting to get back to the Itch. . . I mean, Itzuko-2, so I'm free at your convenience."

He held out his PA, which Sky tapped with hers. She'd now be able to reach him at any time.

"Thank you, Staff Sergeant," the mother superior said before standing back, one hand indicating the hatch.

"I never meant to insult the boy," Sister Keiko said as they walked down the corridor. "We don't have Marines in the Alliance of Free States."

"It's OK, I'm sure. He could have told you. He can face Dictymorphs in combat; I would have assumed that he could face a Jesuit nun."

"You'd be surprised," the woman said with a laugh before pointing down a cross-corridor. "Down this way to the dungeon."

If security was strict at the terminal gate, it was doubly so at the D Lab entrance. The "dungeon" was where the most secure research was done, and that most certainly included the research done on the Dictymorph sample. It took a full two minutes and more scans before she was issued a visitor badge and escorted into the lab itself. Keyshon didn't have the clearance, so he was left outside.

The armed escort and the mother superior led her to an observation room that looked out into a lab room, complete with enough tubes, scanners, and other assorted equipment to make a Hollybolly set designer proud. Sky was more of a compiler of other's research—she was not a lab rat, so she didn't even know the function of even half of what was in there. None of that registered with her at the moment, though. Her attention was laser-focused on the sample on a table in the center of the room, clear raised rails keeping it trapped on top.

Sky had seen functioning Dictymorphs before, and she'd barely survived the meetings. A shudder ran through her. The sample was immediately recognizable as coming from the Dictymorph ecosystem, despite the many differences between it and a full-sized creature.

"Vice-Minister, if I may. I'm the Learned Doke Jameson," an elderly man said, stepping up to stand next to her.

L. Jameson was one of the chief researches on the project, and Sky had long been familiar with his work. He came from the Confed world of Lister, a semi-autonomous planet where "doctor" meant medical doctor, and "learned" was the preferred title for those with academic doctorates.

"Yes, I know who you are," Sky said. "I have to tell you; the report took me by surprise. Before you get into the details, I want to know, how sure are you of this? How sure are *all* of you about this?"

She looked into the learned's eyes as he said, "Very sure. I'd stake my career on it."

"But not one hundred percent."

"Nothing is a hundred percent, Vice-Minister. You know that."

The learned's face was calm, without emotion. Sky stole a look at the mother superior, who simply nodded her agreement.

"OK, Learned Jameson. Tell me, then. How did you come to the conclusion that this was not a juvenile Dictymorph?"

There it was, the reason for her trip. She had to get a feel for the men and women who had uploaded the report. She needed to know before she would lend her weight in support of it. This wasn't about Sky's career. Being wrong could affect the war effort, setting it back and costing countless lives needlessly.

"We have tissue samples of adult Dictymorphs, as you know. We've mapped out their DNA analog. We haven't deciphered it yet, but we know what it looks like. That sample there does not have the same DNA, but is more of a stripped-down version. It is far simpler, and there are huge gaps in it."

"So maybe their DNA develops as the young develop?"

"In all our research, with Terran life and alien life from close to five hundred worlds, in only one, on K-2007, does a native analog of DNA develop as the organism ages."

"So, why can't that be happening here?"

"It could be, but we don't think so. On K-2207, the local DNA develops along existing branches. In this case, those branches simply don't exist."

Sky had read the report, and she already knew what he'd just said. She just wanted to hear his voice as he told her. She wanted to know how confident he was in his beliefs.

"If that thing is not a Dictymorph young, then what is it? The adult Dictymorphs were sure tending them. What are they? The Dictymorph equivalent to a flock of sheep?"

"We don't really know yet. We're working on several trains of thought. One of them is yes, that they are a type of food animal. But even then, so much is missing from the DNA that we doubt that the adults could make much use of the sample bodies as a type of food. It would be too inefficient if it could even be done at all."

Sky absorbed what he'd said. She'd been so sure—everyone had been so sure—that the samples were baby Dictymorphs. They were going to be the Rosetta Stone in unlocking the secrets of the Dictymorphs—unlocked so they could discover how to defeat them.

If they weren't Dictymorph offspring, then what were they? Food animals? Stock animals? Lab rats? The Dictymorph version of a Pomeranian?

"What other ideas are you floating about?"

"Food animals, agricultural pollinators, drug manufacturers . . ."

Humans often used GM biologicals, mostly virus and bacteria, to manufacture drugs and compounds, but she didn't think it was feasible with multi-cellular organisms. Still, they were dealing with an alien being, so they had to consider all possibilities with an open mind.

"I have an idea, Vice-Minister," a voice said from the wall behind her where a dozen men and women were watching.

Sky didn't miss at least half of the others rolling their eyes.

"Malcolm . . ." Learned Jameson started, then trailed off.

Sky caught the look on the mother superior's face. As sure as she was standing there, she was also sure that the woman was pleased by this Malcolm and what he might have to say.

"And what is that idea?" she asked, turning to the young—*very* young—man.

"I think they're batteries," he said, his voice cracking.

"What? Batteries?"

"He's been on this kick," Learned Jameson said. "Can't leave it alone."

"Can he be right?" Sky asked.

"Possibly, but we just don't have enough information to make that kind of conjecture."

"But we do have enough information to suggest they are drug manufacturers?" Sky asked.

"No, not . . ." the learned started before grudgingly nodding his head.

"What is your name?" Sky asked, turning back to the young man.

"Malcolm Orrisy, ma'am."

"Malcolm is a doctoral candidate from Whizzer University," Sister Keiko said, stepping forward. "Dean Wheng suggested that Malcolm be temporarily assigned to the mission."

The pieces began to fall into place. Whizzer was one of the premier schools in human space, but they were noted for not only thinking outside of the box, but usually in an entirely different dimension than where the box was. The fact that he was from Whizzer and didn't have a Ph.D. yet probably rubbed some of the others the wrong way. Everyone else in the room undoubtedly had one or more doctorates, and as Sky well knew, academics could be pricklier about their degrees than the Marines could be about rank.

Sky didn't give a rat's ass about where the young man came from, however. If he had an idea, then she wanted to hear it.

"Explain yourself, Malcolm," she told him.

"Well, as you know, ma'am, the key to a Dictymorph's ability to fight is its stored energy. Deplete that energy enough, and the creature either self-destructs or simply collapses."

He paused, looking at her as if she should have already picked up her point.

"And . . .?" she prompted him.

"Well, we're making military progress against them when we attrit their energy, when we drain or counteract it. If we can shield our soldiers long enough for our energy-sapping weapons, then we can defeat them. We are getting better and better at that."

"Yes, I know how valuable the research has been in enabling our military to take the fight to the enemy," Sky said.

"So, what if they had more energy to spend? There seems to be a limit as to the total amount that an undamaged Dictymorph can hold. But like strap-on fuel tanks on aircraft during long-ago World War Two, if there was something else that could hold the energy, then they could fight longer on a single charge, so to speak."

Malcolm was looking at her eagerly, and she could see that he was trying to will her to agree with him. What he said was true in abstract, but she didn't have anything to suggest that the thing in the lab could act as a "strap-on fuel tank."

"And what makes you think the sample there is a battery?"

"Look at the numbers, ma'am," he said, eagerly rushing forward, PA out for her to see. "A kilogram of human fat contains about 32.2 megajoules. When you consider the combination of tissues in a body, a lean human being has an average of 9.7 megajoules per kilogram.

"A Dictymorph, on the other hand, has much more energy. We've never been able to calculate the entire body, but from the fragments we've examined, they look to be on the order of ninety to a hundred megajoules per kilogram."

Sky already knew that, and it made sense given that they "fired" light weapons which put out huge amounts of energy.

"But look at this!" he shouted, unable to control his excitement. "That sample in there, it's nothing but energy. We're talking close to nine-hundred-and-eighty megajoules per kilogram. It is an energy bank."

"So, it could be an organic bomb of some sort, designed to detonate among human fighters," she said.

Learned Jameson nodded at that, a self-satisfied smile making a tiny appearance.

"Yes, that's possible, but not efficient. There are no mechanisms that we can discern in the body that would allow for a rapid release. Rather, the most significant means of moving the energy are these structures, which, when broken down, look remarkably like Fesson lines."

Sky looked at the diagram. The structures did have a similar composition to the highly efficient Fesson lines, which transmitted power over long distances.

"It's intuitively obvious to even the most casual observer," he said, then added a perfunctory "Ma'am."

Sky looked up from the PA at the young man. He had a look that spanned from hopeful that she would buttress his contention to what she took as scorn that her simple mind couldn't grasp his own hold on the truth.

I can see why no one here likes you. You're kind of a pompous ass, aren't you?

Still, Sky needed to know just what that blob of Dictymorph tissue was, and she didn't care if Malcolm was a social reject or not. If he was right, then human and Klethos-kind needed to know.

Unlike the more hidebound Klethos, who without human intervention had been rather static during their long war with the Dictymorphs, the enemy had shown an ability to adjust their tactics to meet the new human-Klethos force. They had to understand that the human and Klethos' current focus was to drain each of their soldier's energy stores.

Sky didn't know if Malcolm was correct, but it made sense in the larger picture. If that thing in there was a battery of sorts, then it was a logical course of action for the Dictymorphs to take. Such an advancement on their part could make them far better fighters than they already were, and that would be a serious setback to the war, possibly one that couldn't be overcome.

But with every change also came opportunity.

She had some of the brightest minds in human space standing in the room with her, some minds that probably eclipsed hers—maybe even that young, arrogant student still standing in front of her. She knew it was her job to guide the team, to harness their brainpower.

"Learned Jameson, I want to reconvene in twenty minutes in a fully connected conference room, big enough for everyone in this room now and anyone else I might call in. Take half of your people and get them working on how to disapprove Mr. Orrisy's theory."

Malcolm stepped forward, his mouth gaping like a goldfish at her audacity in refusing his . . . not *theory*, to him, she knew, but grasp of the simple facts.

"The other half will focus on proving that the sample is, in fact, a battery, as Mr. Orrisy believes."

Learned Jameson hesitated, and Sky could see that he was wondering if she had the authority to tell him what to do. What he'd thought of as a courtesy brief had just taken a different turn.

"I am not acting as a Federation vice-minister in this but as a Special Advisor to the secretary-general," she said, trying to put as much gravitas as she could into her voice.

He still hesitated, glancing at the others for support.

"If you would prefer, I'll call the secretary-general right now and make that an official order. It's 0234 in the morning in Brussels," she said, checking the time, "but I'm sure he won't mind being woken for this."

His eyes widened at that, and then he hastily said, "No, we don't need to wake the secretary-general. And we do have a space for that, CF-202. Dr. Kristenov, if you could go get Horatio to open it up for us?" he added, turning toward a man who was with the others that were standing alongside the back wall.

Sky stood back, her heart fluttering in her chest. She was not used to forcing her will, preferring to rely instead on concurrence as her management style. But this was too important. She knew that they had to consider the battery theory—one that felt right to her on a gut level. So, if she had to "kick ass and take names," as the Marines said, then she would.

Is some of that Marines stuff sinking in on me?

The thought that she, of all people, could absorb anything from the Marines was surprising, but also stroked her ego just the tiniest bit.

Her ship was still docked, waiting for her departure, but the situation had changed, and she had to be where she could best manage the research.

"Keyshon," she said, pulling him up on her PA. "Tell the ship's captain to stand down and arrange for billeting. We're going to be here for a while."

Chapter 6
Hondo

"I'm sorry about the award," Major Worthington said. "It isn't right, but that's the way it is."

"No problem, sir. I understand," Hondo said.

And he did understand . . . sort of. Everything that had happened on their mission, and then here on the station, was highly classified. So, what he and Ben had accomplished was classified, as well. The two of them couldn't very well be put up for an award, which would be a matter of public record, and still keep what they'd done a secret from the public.

What he didn't understand was why the secrecy in the first place. Did the powers that be think that there were human spies, trying to dig out information to feed to the Grubs? That didn't make sense. Hondo rather thought that every advance, every advantage, should be promulgated as widely as possible. The public's perception of the war now was of an invincible force that was on the verge of wiping out humanity.

Just two weeks ago, a panic-induced riot killed thousands on Emerson when some pranksters floated a Grub-shaped drone above Storytown. People were on edge, on the brink of cracking. They should be calmed down, he thought, and not kept in the dark.

And he shouldn't be kept in the dark, either. He'd caught bits and pieces that what he and Ben had snatched was not a baby Grub but something else. However, when he'd asked what it was, he was told he wasn't cleared for that level of information. Even worse, when the major told him that another team had snatched one, too, and that Grub-whatever was at another research facility, he'd been told that he wasn't cleared for anything more on that, either. So, they thought he'd turn spy for the Grubs, too?

Hondo was sick and tired of *Golden Happiness Station*. *Golden Misery Station* was more like it. And finally, he was going to leave, to get back to the Itch and people he understood. Only a third of the personnel on the small camp out in the mountains were Marines, but he felt more at home with the New Budapest Rangers, the Confed SpecOps, and hell, even the Brotherhood seraphim, than he did with all the civilians on the station. He felt more akin to the Klethos.

"Well, thanks for everything, sir. I wouldn't have survived the eggheads," he said.

"Worse than a Grub, huh?" the major asked, a smile cracking his face. "At least you're getting out of here."

"Hell, sir, that's why they pay you the big bucks."

"I'd give up half of my credits to get back to the fleet, but you know what they say about the two worthless ranks in the Corps, right?"

"Yes, sir, I do. So, I know you gotta take what they give you."

The old saying was that the two worthless ranks in the Corps both wore gold on their collars. A second lieutenant, with his or her gold bar, was too green, too inexperienced, to be much good. A major, with the gold oak leaf, was between ranks, too senior to be a company commander and too junior to command a battalion. Hondo figured that majors were stuffed into any staff or liaison job that the detailers could find until—and if—they were promoted to lieutenant colonel and could get back to what Marines did—close with and destroy the enemy.

"Yeah, I have to take it, but not forever. I've got two-hundred-and-twenty-six days and a wake-up, and I'm off of this floating tin can."

Golden Happiness Station had only been in existence for a few months, so if the major had 226 days left, then he must have gotten here right at the beginning. Hondo felt a pang of sympathy for the man.

"Better you than me, sir," he said, bending to pick up his seabag with his left hand, his right hand out to shake the major's.

And he dropped the seabag.

"Your new hand still doing that vibration thing?" the major asked, concern in his voice.

"Yes, sir. When I get the tips of the little finger and the thumb too close together. Doctor Jay-Aye says it's a feedback loop problem, but he's not a *lab mechanic*, so he can't fix it."

Hondo emphasized the phrase "lab mechanic" to mimic the scorn Dr. Josief-Anderson had used.

"No, that stick-up-his-ass wouldn't stoop so low as to do a real job, would he?"

"Why Major, I'm surprised at you, besmirching the good doctor's name like that," Hondo said, breaking out into laughter.

He was concerned about the vibration, though. He'd gotten used to the hand, but the vibration was not normal. He could even hear a small hum as it vibrated. He knew that until that was fixed, he wouldn't be considered combat effective.

"Well, if you want, Staff Sergeant, I can force the issue and make him fix it. It should only take a few weeks, I'm sure," he said.

"Oh, hell no, sir. I wouldn't put you through the hassle. That's my ride there," he said, pointing over his shoulder with his thumb at the boarding gate. "I'm off to Holcomb Station, and they'll fix it there."

"Are you sure? I hate to send you off like that," the major said, and for a moment, Hondo thought he was serious before he caught the smile and twinkle in his eyes.

I guess majors like to give people shit, too, just like enlisted. We aren't that different.

"With all due respect, sir, if I could, I would show you how my fake hand works right now, especially the middle finger, but it would probably start vibrating, and I don't want anyone to think that's an invitation to come sit on it."

The major broke out into a deep, resounding laugh, then smacked Hondo on the shoulder.

"Fair enough, Staff Sergeant, and with all due respect back to you, you better get your ass onboard your ship, or you will be stuck here with me, sharing the misery."

Hondo had never given a major shit before. As a junior Marine, a major was so high above him that he was in a different universe. But here, among civilians, it was the Marine connection that carried the most weight. He held out his hand again, which the major took.

"Fair winds and following seas, Staff Sergeant. You did good, you and your Klethos. You may not have gotten another medal to go with your Navy Cross, but the commandant himself knows what you did."

"Thank you, sir, and you take care."

Hondo turned and walked through the gate, onto the ship, and then let himself be guided to his small stateroom. It wasn't until the ship undocked that he let out a sigh of relief that he was leaving *Golden Misery Station*.

Chapter 7

Skylar

"These figures, they don't make sense," Malcolm Orrisy said, his brows furrowed in confusion.

Sky almost took pleasure in that. The arrogant young man could be uber-annoying, and he needed a little comeuppance. However, everyone was shocked by the numbers, numbers which suggested the D-cell, as they had started to call the sample, could provide much more energy than previously suggested, enough, even, to double a Dictymorph's energy reserves. Orrisy had initially presented "hard" data that stated a D-cell could only increase a Dictymorph's energy reserves by 62%.

None of that made any sense. Energy was energy, the same anywhere in the known universe. But the organic transmission system in the D-cell seemingly multiplied the real energy not only available, but that could be transferred as well. There was essentially no transmission loss.

"Do Taterville's results match ours?" Sky asked.

"Within two percent," Jameson answered.

Over the last three days, the research was lending credence to Orrisy's theory, something he'd been subtly lording over the rest of the team. There was one other D-cell in human hands, at an unobtrusive lab in Taterville, on Orion Amalgamated 2. The two labs were linked, and the Taterville data reflected what they'd observed here on *Golden Happiness*. Things were worse than they'd thought.

Sky leaned back in her chair, eyes closed with her face pointed to the overhead. Much of the research findings had frankly gone over her head, particularly with regards to the physical aspects of transmission, but she didn't have to be an expert in every discipline. She was the secretary-general's representative at the scene, and it was up to her to manage the team, not take the lead in any single aspect of the research.

In her heart, Sky was still a scientist, someone pushing the boundaries of human knowledge. But she knew her place in life had changed. She might not like to be a manager, a bureaucrat, but that was what she was. And she was suited for it, much as she hated to admit it. It took someone with a scientific bent, someone who could understand the concepts in order to know in which direction to steer things.

She opened her eyes and sat up. Twenty-two people were standing there, waiting for her commands.

"If we get another D-cell, we'll run a Yamamori test," she said, noting the smile on Dr. Gustav.

The Yamamori test would take a D-cell down to its component atoms, destroying it, but giving a definitive figure as to the number of joules it contained. He'd been pushing it for the last day, but Sky wouldn't authorize the destruction of either of the two D-cells they held.

"But for now, whether it offers an additional sixty-two or a hundred-and-three percent doesn't matter. We need to know how to counteract them. Learned Jameson, let's brainstorm here about how we can neutralize the process. Get Taterville to focus on how to physically remove a D-cell from its Dictymorph.

"And if anyone else has any ideas, bring them forward. We've got to consider every option. Any questions?"

No one said a world, so she added, "Then let's get going, people. We've got a war to win."

HOLCOLM STATION

Chapter 8
Hondo

Security was tighter on *Holcomb Station* than on a commercial station, and Hondo waited anxiously for his orders to be verified. He didn't understand the red tape—he'd arrived on a Navy ship-of-the-line, he'd been scanned to prove he was who he said he was, and Marines stationed down on Aegis 2 could come and go as they pleased. Since he wasn't assigned to the sector, however, they had to check to make sure he was authorized to be there. Finally, he was cleared to proceed and told to report to the station's physical therapy clinic for billeting.

Hondo could have picked any of fifty such clinics, but he wanted Holcolm Station. He'd be there for the next week or so while refinements were made to his prosthetic before going back to the Itch to prepare for his next mission. The reason he'd chosen *Holcolm* was waiting for him as he passed into the station proper.

"Hey, Hondo!" Lauren shouted, waving a hand.

All his frustration over the delay vanished like the morning dew as he rushed around the barriers used to funnel passengers and took Lauren into a surprisingly strong hug. Thankfully, she hugged him back with equal fervor.

"Get a room," someone said from behind him. Hondo was in too good a mood to turn and beat whoever it was to a pulp.

"Let me see," Lauren said, breaking the hug and lifting his left forearm so she could see his hand. "Cammo pattern. So Marine Corps."

"Well, you know me. Now anyone who sees me will think I'm just a bush," he said, raising his hand and covering his face.

"Right," she said, then pushed the hand down to give him a quick kiss. "So, what's your schedule? When do you report in?"

"The guy at receiving said to check in right away," he said, noting the quick look of what he hoped was disappointment on her face. "But my orders say tomorrow, and I never disobey written orders."

She burst into a smile that made his heart want to sing.

"Well, in that case, I've got a reservation made at the Navy Lodge, unless you're bound and determined to get a rack in the barracks."

"Well, the Lodge sounds good, and maybe you can come see me in the morning after I wake up."

She gave him a good hard shot to this bicep and said, "Oh, I'll see you all right."

Lauren and Hondo had slept together a couple of times: the first time after a hard night of partying, and then the second just before he left for Tarawa to commence recon training. There had been a lot of water under the bridge since then, though, and Hondo hadn't wanted to assume anything. But it looked like things were good to go.

He hesitated. What he'd thought before would be half-funny and half-sexy in the safety of distance now made him nervous. He wondered if he should leave well enough alone. She obviously planned to spend the night with him, and he didn't want to wreck that.

"Well, do you want to stop at Piccalo's first?" she asked, knowing that was his favorite restaurant on the station. She was standing there, looking at him and waiting for an answer.

Come on, you freaking chicken-shit. Just be a man.

He reached out with his left arm, prosthetic hand against her butt, and pulled her in for another kiss. As their lips met, he brought the tips of his thumb and little finger together, triggering the vibration. Lauren jumped, but *into* him, not away, giving a little squeal that she quickly smothered.

"Oh, my goodness, Hondo. You are full of surprises," she whispered into his ear. "Is that part of the package?"

"It's a malfunction. They'll fix that tomorrow."

"Tomorrow? So, it won't . . . do what it's doing after today?
In that case, my boy, pizza will wait. You and I are going to the
room right now!"

Hondo's face blushed hot and red as she almost dragged him
off, one hand firmly grasping his prosthetic like she didn't plan on
ever letting go.

DESIGNATED PLANET D42

Chapter 9
Hondo

"Do they have the D-cells?" Hondo asked, as he glassed the valley below.

Ben grunted and checked the readouts before saying, "They could be. The readings are inconclusive."

Hondo focused on the backs of the Grubs where the D-cells were supposed to be, but at 20 klicks, even the Zeiss Magna-40s couldn't discern enough detail.

"Where's the dragonfly?" he asked.

"Give it another four minutes, and we should be able to pick up something."

The mission so far had been a bust. When Navy Viper surveillance had confirmed that there were Grubs with D-cells on the planet, there were only two Interrecon teams on the Itch: his team and Colour Sergeant Howell and Horace. Byron and Horace had been the other team to successfully snatch up a D-cell, and both were back on the Itch, going through debriefs and preparing to go back out again.

Both teams had been rushed to the latest Grub incursion, laden with equipment that Hondo barely understood. He didn't have to understand them, however, he only had to know how to operate them. The two teams had been drilled on their setup and operation by a team of civilians back on *Golden Misery* before they donned their podsuits and made the transit.

They had landed ten days ago, just two days before the Brotherhood task force landed. Byron and Horace were over 6,000 klicks away at a second front, inserted in the path of another, smaller concentrations of Grubs. Each team hoped to be in place and recording during a battle.

Hondo and Ben had, in fact, been in place for the first battle, but those Grubs didn't have D-cells. The two of them had managed to get their equipment set up just in time, then they'd watched the Sons of the Brotherhood lose a hard-fought fight to the Grubs and been forced to retreat.

It had been hard to watch from the safety of the high ground, but their equipment was the reason for the season, and they couldn't jeopardize it.

Half-way around the planet, Byron and Horace weren't having much better luck. In that AOR, the first Grubs were the 1.0 versions as well. The Sons of the Brotherhood had a little better luck in that engagement, suffering heavy losses, but managing to turn back the Grubs.

With the human forces in their AOR retreating, Hondo and Ben had to rush along the ridgeline, lugging almost 400 kg of equipment. Even with his kinesthetic strap-on, which helped shoulder the load, Hondo knew they'd never have been able to keep up without Ben's superior strength. As it was, they'd barely made it to the high ground above where the Sons were digging in to make a stand.

Hondo knew their equipment had been thrown together from existing lab instruments and were not anything designed for field use. They were making do, but if this was going to be a thing, then they had to reduce the weight and make it sturdier for field use, something Hondo had already reported back.

He shifted his gaze from the advancing Grubs to the Sons of the Brotherhood below. They were in a flurry of activity, digging in. They could just about engage the Grubs already, but they'd wait to hit them when the Grubs were about five or six klicks out.

Until the arrival of the Grubs, naval battles took place covering hundreds of thousands of klicks. Ground troops typically engaged from 50 to 60 klicks out, and air and naval gunfire hit the enemy whenever it could.

Now, the Grubs would knock any naval ship out of space if it engaged. Aircraft didn't fare much better, and the weapons designed to engage the Grubs had a very limited range, which fortunately was just about the same as the range in which the Grubs fired upon humans and Klethos. In a very real sense, it was ironic, that with the most modern weapons available to infantry, current battles were conducted from five klicks and closer.

The Sons probably had twenty minutes until the battle commenced. Soon, many of those figures he watched would be dead. It was possible that all of them would be killed.

The Sons of the Brotherhood were an enigma to Hondo. They were an extremely humanistic group, asserting that as man was made in God's image, only man was the rightful heir to the universe. They'd risen from the varied groups who'd been prime movers in the Brotherhood's withdrawal from the alliance with the Klethos—groups calling the Klethos the seeds of Satan. After Destiny was attacked by the Grubs and the Brotherhood rejoined the alliance, they hadn't protested, as might have been expected.

On the small world of Hydros, a thirteen-year-old girl had a vision that the Klethos, far from being the tools of Satan, were rather warrior angels sent from God to serve humankind. The vision swept like a virus through the undernet, and the Sons of the Brotherhood was born, men determined to right the wrong of initially opposing God's will. Following their modern-day Jeanne d'Arc, they were eager to face the Grubs, even to die, to prove their faith.

And down below the two Interrecon teammates, there was a small figure who strode back and forth along the FLOT, the forward line of troops, waving her arms in encouragement, dressed in what looked to be a simple brown robe. It had to be Celeste Moran, the girl who had the vision. She was out there, in harm's way.

Hondo respected bravery, he respected loyalty to a cause. He'd served with Marines who'd sacrificed their lives to save their brother and sister Marines. Heck, he'd been ready to sacrifice his own life on more than one occasion. But the Sons were zealots, in his opinion, and he didn't trust them. If Celeste had another vision, then they could turn on the Klethos in an instant. He had to give them grudging credit for standing tall, but basing everything on the vision of a young girl made no sense to him.

When Hondo mentioned his feelings to Ben, the Klethos asked how different their religion was from what he called the religion of the Marine Corps. Hondo had snapped at him, saying that the two were different, and stormed away. Deep inside, though, he knew there might be a little bit of truth to what Ben had said. And that was part of what made the Corps what it was: the best fighting force known to man.

"The Grubs have the S-Po," Ben said, his frill rippling as he studied one of the many readouts.

"What? Esspoe?" Hondo asked, jerking his thoughts back to the here and now.

"S-Po, as in the letter 'S' followed by 'po,'" he said, turning to look at Hondo.

"What the hell are you talking about, Ben?"

"Well, I've been thinking. 'D-cell' doesn't make much sense. It's not a cell, and what is the 'D?' But it is a supplemental power pod. 'S' for 'supplemental,' and 'po' for 'power.'"

"What? They called it a D-cell on *Golden Misery*, so what's wrong with that?"

"It's not very descriptive, is it?" Ben asked.

"And your S-Po is? 'Supplemental power?'"

The Klethos beak was inflexible, but Hondo swore he saw it somehow twisted into a smile as Ben said, "No, but 'shitpod' is, and that's descriptive, right?"

"What is with you, Ben? 'Supplemental power,' 'S-Po,' and now you're saying 'shitpod?' Are you high?" he asked before it hit him.

Shitpod. S-Po.

That was exactly the kind of nickname a Marine or sailor would come up with, and like all good nicknames, it had two interpretations: a "clean" one for the O's, and a real one for the enlisted.

Hondo broke out into a laugh. If he'd had any doubt before, he knew now for a fact that the Klethos had a sense of humor, and one not too different from human's.

"Shit, Ben, we're going to make a Marine out of you yet. Fucking 'S-Po.' Whatever you call them, what matters is that those

Grubs down there have them, so maybe we can get the readings now.

"I'm going to inform the captain," he told Ben, then opened the comms.

It had been surprisingly difficult to initiate communications with the commander of the force in their AO, just another example of the difficulties in meshing units. Eventually, though, he had an open commercial line that he could access.

"Captain Destafney, this is Staff Sergeant McKeever," he said as if anyone else was going to be using this circuit.

"What is it, Staff Sergeant?" the captain asked. "We're rather busy at the moment, so, can you keep it short?"

"Yes, sir. I just want to tell you, the Grubs have the S- . . . the D-cells, so please, keep up the fight until we can start to reach energy depletion levels."

There was a moment of silence, and Hondo wondered if the comms had been cut, but then the captain said, "Don't tell me how to fight, Staff Sergeant. We understand God's will, and we are ready to follow it. You and your measurements are irrelevant, so you do what you're going to do and leave the fighting to us."

This time Hondo knew the comms had been cut, but by the captain. There was nothing he could do about it but hope that the Sons would fight long enough for them to gather all the data they needed to uplink.

"You didn't say 'S-Po,'" Ben said, almost accusingly.

Hondo rolled his eyes, and then said, "Just worry about our mission, Ben."

He checked the status lights on all nine instruments. Everything was green. Five of them were already recording readings, which were feeding the uplink to the tiny satellite in geosynchronous orbit halfway between Byron's team's position and theirs. The data was on a twinned hadron feed back to the real world, so if something took the two of them out, whatever had already been gathered wouldn't be lost.

Hondo looked at the numbers flashing on the readouts. They meant absolutely jack shit to him. He just hoped they would be worth the lives that were about to be lost.

A flash caught his attention as it zipped up the valley, just about level with them. He looked up to see a Brotherhood Cherubim, bearing down on the Grubs at Mach speeds. The plane was two klicks down the valley before the sound reached him.

Whatever he might think of the Sons of Brotherhood battalion, the Cherubim was one of the finest manned atmospheric crafts ever made. Hondo stood up to get a better view as it streaked towards the enemy. Green pulses reached out to splash the Grubs at the same time that three light tendrils reached up and converged, a bright beam flashing from the confluence to hit the Cherubim.

Instead of breaking off, the pilot kept flying, his plasma cannon in rapid fire mode as an aura of light surrounded him.

"Come on, break contact," Hondo muttered.

He didn't know the specifics of the Cherubim shielding, but it couldn't stand up to the converged beam. Hondo didn't know how any aircraft could last even a minute—to his eyes, the beam was the same type that destroyed naval ships-of-the-line.

The pilot fired missiles, which flew for only an instant before they skewed to the side, knocked out of action. Then, with a flash, the Cherubim exploded, parts shotgunning out as they arched down to crash onto the ground, still ten klicks from the Grub FLET, the Forward Line of Enemy Troops.

"Well, shit," Hondo said. "What a waste."

"Why a waste? His plasma cannon has certainly diminished the Grub energy stores," Ben said. "Look, all of our instruments are recording."

Hondo gave a quick look, and Ben was right. All nine of the instruments were now uplinking data.

"That Cherubim was one of the last two left on the planet. Now they have only one left."

"But what are they for, if not to fight?" Ben asked.

Ben was right, but Hondo thought a better tactic would be to fire and then break contact in order to come back with another pass. The pilot was almost certainly not a Sons of the Brotherhood—the Cherubim took quite some training to master, and so it would have been flown by a professional air guard pilot. Yet he'd still commenced on what he had to have known was a suicide run.

Like those poor saps down there.

The Brotherhood battalion numbered about 1,400 host, and they faced over 200 Grubs. Even without the shitpods, those were pretty steep odds. With the extra energy stores, Hondo wasn't sure how the Brotherhood fighters could hope to survive. They would have to retreat. He just hoped the sensors he and Ben had man-and-Klethos-packed into position would be able to gather enough data before that happened.

Hondo's pulse was climbing, his pre-fight nerves rising, as the Grubs closed the distance. This was normal for him, something that usually disappeared before the first shot was fired. But not this time. He stood up behind the arrayed instruments and started pacing, full of nervous energy.

Ben gave him an inscrutable look, but Hondo didn't bother to say anything. He knew what was wrong. The warrior Hondo was aching to be released, but that wasn't going to happen. He and Ben were to remain quiet and unseen while the battle unfolded, and that went entirely against his nature. He was a fighter, a brawler, pure and simple. That is what he was, what defined him.

After twenty more minutes, there was a flash that lit up the valley and hills like lightening. Hondo stepped back up and went prone, binos in hand. Below him, the battalion had commenced fire with their plasma cannons, blasting measured bursts into the oncoming Grubs.

Plasma was not as effective as meson beams against the Grubs. Plasma cannons required more power, and their range was much shorter, but they were simpler, cheaper, and fired a more spectacular-looking shot. The green bolts (the signature of Brotherhood weaponry) reached out, splashing the first line of Grubs. Bathed in this aura, the Grubs glowed like fireflies—huge, inimical fireflies, but fireflies just the same.

They didn't falter, but kept advancing. The four cannons slowed down their volleys, two firing first, and then the other two. Hondo glassed to where he'd seen the generators emplaced, but they were completely underground now. That would give them more protection from the Grubs, but it also meant that they were there for the duration. The Sons could not retreat with them. It was either defeat the Grubs or abandon the most powerful weapon in their T/E.

Their dragonfly had been bird-dogging the Grub advance, and Hondo pulled down his monocle, linking into the drone. One-hundred-and-ninety-three Grubs were arrayed in six loose lines as they moved to contact. From the feed, it looked as if only two ranks were being affected by the plasma beams. The first rank was getting lit up something fierce, and the second had some strikes, but the third looked untouched.

While Hondo was observing, tendrils of light reached out and *over* the first two ranks before bending back down to hit the Sons of the Brotherhood.

Shit, they've never done that before! Hondo thought as he checked the dragonfly's uplink.

It was as if the Grubs in the third rank were providing covering fire instead of simply the nearest Grub firing at whatever it could. If this was a new tactic, then the command needed to see this.

The uplink was strong. With the satellite above, the task force command would be seeing this in real time.

He flipped up his monocle, switching back to his binos, and shifted back to the host. The light tendrils were playing along the Brotherhood frontage. Hondo could see the shielding glow with energy expenditure, but they were holding for the moment—until two of the tendrils seemed to converge and strike one of the cannons. The gun had been dug in so only the tip of the projector was exposed, but that was enough. There was a flash, and the cannon went silent.

This was also something new. The Grubs had always been able to merge their tendrils, but the juncture was usually near them, and then the larger, more coherent beam would shoot off to take down a ship, aircraft, or weapons emplacement. This time, the tendrils converged almost onto the target. The tendrils had always seemed analogous to a stream of water being directed from a garden hose, controlled by the Grub "holding the hose." This time, the tendrils reacted at the end of the stream. , Hondo thought that they had to be being directed from that point.

A volley of missiles streaked out, some flying high to come down onto the Grubs, others streaking along barely a meter off the ground. This was a typical Brotherhood tactic, designed to force defenses to spread out their defensive fires. Hondo didn't think it would make much difference to the Grubs. The missiles started exploding against the first two lines, but as with the cannons, the enemy didn't falter.

More and more light tendrils reached from the back five ranks, all converging onto the cannons and the forward elements of the Brotherhood defense. Two more of the cannons went up, overcome by the incoming fire, leaving one to send out pulse after pulse of plasma beams.

"Hey, Ben, don't they have six cannons on their T/E?" Hondo asked as he tried to remember.

Ben just shrugged. The Klethos sometimes had a lack of curiosity about details that could drive Hondo crazy. He was sure, though, that there had been six of them on the T/E that he'd read. He pulled his monocle back down and queried his AI. In an instant, the T/E was displayed, and yes, the 4th Host Battalion had six GS-406 plasma cannons. Hondo couldn't see any more on the battlefield.

Maybe they left two behind when they retreated last time?

At that moment, the last of the four that had been firing was taken out in a mountain of sparks that shot up 70 meters into the air. There was a flurry of motion as bodies scrambled clear. Two of them dropped as they were touched by Grub tendrils.

Perversely, with the cannons gone, the distance had to close before the soldiers could employ their next line of Grub-specific weapons. The newest version of the sonic projector had a greater range than the one that Hondo had first seen used on Destiny, but it was still limited to about 300 meters. The grappling hooks, which pierced Grub skin to deliver a charge, had a max effective range of only 400 meters. The host was delivering sporadic fire, but Hondo thought most of that was from automatic positions as the soldiers hugged the bottom of their fighting holes while the Grubs swept the positions with their tendrils.

"Any sign of the Grubs getting low on energy?" Hondo asked Ben.

The Klethos hooked his upper left arm, thumb pointing at the instruments, and said, "Those might tell, but I can't read them."

The front rank of Grubs, 28 of them in all, had taken some heavy pounding. They had to have expended a lot of energy in their shielding, even if they hadn't been firing. The third rank of 24 Grubs was doing the bulk of the firing, but they hadn't taken much in the way of Brotherhood hits. Which rank would be the most depleted was the 64,000-credit question.

"They're getting close," Hondo said as the first rank closed in on the Brotherhood's forward elements.

He kept waiting for the host to open fire, to start dropping Grubs, but they kept silent.

They can't have been taken out already. They've been dug in.

For all the high-tech shielding, one of the most effective ways to weather a Grub light tendril was to put a meter of dirt between a soldier and the impact spot. Hugging the bottom of a fighting hole made it difficult to fire back with anything other than automatic weapons systems, but it kept soldiers alive.

And then the Grubs were within the lines, sweeping through the host as if it wasn't there. Automatic weapons positions were knocked out, and outgoing fire dwindled away to nothing. The second and third ranks passed the FLOT—and the Grubs slowed down as if not sure what they should do.

"Hell, we're not going to get any of the bastards depleted," Hondo said.

He didn't know why the surviving host were kissing the bottom of their holes. They should have fired their FPF, the mass of Final Protective Fires designed to stop and enemy in its tracks. Maybe the Grubs would keep advancing and bypass those dug-in soldiers, but they should have at least made an effort.

Ben's frill was flattened along his shoulders, a true sign that he was disgusted, too. Not figthing was unfathomable, and not just to a Marine.

The entire Grub advance slowed down. A few tendrils of light reached out and almost caressed the ground as if trying to find a target, poking and prodding like a moray in a coral reef.

Then the entire position lit up. Green plasma erupted from under the ground, dirt pulverized into dust and rising in the air as one beam struck the flank of the first rank of Grubs, and the second hitting the third rank. Through his binos, Hondo saw heads appear as hundreds of grappling hooks flew through the air to strike Grub bodies. Four soldiers jumped out of their holes, rushing forward with pikes just as one of their own plasma beams swept across them, reducing each soldier into his component atoms.

"Fuck! They're firing the FPF on their own freaking positions!" Hondo said, his voice low in amazement.

The host weren't hiding, hoping to be bypassed. They waited until the Grubs were within their lines and at extremely close range. The two cannons Hondo had noted had been dug in and buried, trap-door spiders ready to spring their ambushes.

Hondo stepped up to the edge of the drop-off, standing exposed as he took in the scene. Two, then three Grubs were knocked out as the rest sprayed light tendrils in what Hondo would swear was panic. Another Grub exploded in a burst of energy, taking with it another half- dozen soldiers who had closed in to attack it.

More and more combat-suited soldiers appeared from fighting holes, firing every weapon in their arsenal. For a moment, Hondo wanted to shout out in joy. Despite all the odds, it looked as if the soldiers might prevail.

But then one of the cannons was knocked out, followed a few moments later by the second. The Grubs seemed to gather themselves, and instead of a flurry of aimless tendrils, they looked to be more organized, more focused. Soldiers started falling. The straight infantry was swept aside, and the 150 or so combat-suited soldiers started falling. The Brotherhood Malakh was a good piece of gear, almost as good as a PICS, but they couldn't stand up to the fusillade after fusillade of Grub fire.

Ben stepped up to stand beside Hondo, his focus on the battle below. His neck frill was fully erect.

"There's nothing we can do, Ben," Hondo said, reaching out to place his hand on Ben's lower left forearm.

Ben violently jerked his arm aside, and for a moment, Hondo thought his teammate was going to lash out at him. But then his blazing eyes dimmed ever so slightly, and he made the cocked Klethos-nod to signify his assent.

He knew how Ben felt. It was just wrong for the two of them to stand there, safe and sound klicks away, as the battalion was getting slaughtered. It wasn't as they could do much, but he felt like they had to do *something*. They had their mission, however, and that had to be their priority.

"Look," Ben said, pointing with both right arms.

Hondo pulled up his binos and immediately saw what Ben had caught. A small, brown-robed figure, holding a pike that was way too big for her, had emerged from a fighting hole near the rear of the defensive position. Behind her, an honor guard of eight soldiers followed. All nine of them were charging the Grubs, the nearest about 100 meters away. The girl's mouth was open in a scream, and Hondo could see the intensity in her eyes. This was someone who knew her purpose in life and was certain of what she had to do.

"No . . ." Hondo started, instinctively reaching for his M96.

A glancing touch of a light tendril swept through the group, dropping little Celeste into a heap on the ground. Three of her bodyguards dropped as well, but the other five kept charging.

Hondo lowered the binos. He didn't need to see any more.

Within five minutes, it was over. There was no Brotherhood fire. The Grubs milled about for a few more minutes, and then as one, they oriented further down the valley and moved out.

They left eight of their own behind, though, and Hondo prayed that their instruments had captured the data that the science-types needed.

That data had come at a very high price.

GOLDEN HAPPINESS STATION

Chapter 10
Skylar

"And using the Shvartzman Regression?" Sky asked.

"Within two percent. The D-cells look to increase the energy stores by ninety-six-point-three percent. That's within two-percent of the previous calculations," Learned Jameson said.

"Do our figures match Taterville's?"

"To six sig figs, yes."

Sky wasn't surprised by that answer. They were reading the same data, after all, so it should have matched to the six significant figures. She looked at the rest of the gathered team. The data they'd used had come at the cost of 1400 lives. She felt a wave of guilt over that, a wave she'd had to push down with a force of will. But as everyone had agreed, they couldn't effectively come up with countermeasures until the understood what they were facing. Now, armed with numbers, they could begin to engineer the various ideas that they'd developed.

"Well, then. I think we can accept the figures. But remember, we can't assume a static situation. The Dictymorphs have proven to be able to adjust, and these D-cells could be the one-point-oh version. So, we need to engineer in a cushion."

There were a few nods, but no one had anything to add.

"Then let's knuckle down and push on. Everyone's got a project, and I want briefs on how the findings are going to affect them. First brief in . . ." she paused, checking the time, ". . .in twelve hours."

There were a few eye-rolls at that. Twelve hours was barely enough time to open a file in the universe of scientific research, but lives were at stake. Fourteen hundred lives had been lost to get them the data they needed, so if they had to eat at their labs, if they had to go without sleep, then so be it.

No one moved, so Sky put a little steel into her voice and repeated, "I said twelve hours. You don't have time to stand here gawking. Asses and elbows, people, asses and elbows."

DESIGNATED PLANET D42

Chapter 11
Hondo

Hondo sat on top of the square UUV-461, one of the instruments—whose purpose was totally lost on him—elbows on his knees, chin resting in his hands. The battle below was over, and the Grubs were long gone. There were a few wisps of smoke rising from the battlefield, but if he didn't use his binos or monocle, he could imagine that nothing had happened.

"Any human forces, any human forces, come in," he passed again for the umpteenth time.

As before, there was no answer.

He and Ben were waiting for orders. The needed data had been collected. They could be given the recall, or they could be given orders to find another battle to observe. Without any human forces anywhere near them, that might be easier said than done, though.

Ben lay prone on the dirt, in the trance-like state that served the Klethos instead of sleep. The fingers of his upper hands drummed the slightest of tattoos on his chest.

Fuck it, Hondo thought, jumping off the instrument.

"Watch this stuff," he told Ben.

"Where are you going?" Ben asked, sitting up, instantly awake.

"Down there."

"Why?"

"There might be someone alive down there. Or someone who can be resurrected."

"Our orders are to remain with the gear, Hondo," Ben said, his voice steady and calm.

"Since when are you Klucks so worried about orders?" Hondo snapped.

"Klucks" was a derogatory term for Klethos, and Hondo knew that he was just taking out his frustration on his teammate. He didn't apologize despite that.

"It is not me who is acting out of the ordinary. It is you humans who value following the orders given to you."

"So, you don't have a problem with me going down there, then," he said, as a statement of fact.

"I will go with you."

Hondo looked at his teammate, and then at the instruments.

"Why the hell not? If someone comes along and steals this stuff, they can take it out of my salary."

"So, you will remain a Marine for the next 90 years, then, to pay off their value?" Ben asked in a deadpan voice.

Hondo stared at him for a moment, but he couldn't tell if Ben was joking or not. With a shrug, he turned and started down the hill, not caring if the Klethos followed him or not. He crashed down, letting gravity speed him down the rocks and scree that covered the slope. It took him four minutes to get to the bottom of the hill, then another ten to hike to the battlefield.

There was surprisingly little left of the 1400 Sons of the Brotherhood. Many had been atomized. He and Ben found body parts, but it took another ten minutes to find a whole body. The soldier was dead, and missing most of his legs, but otherwise, he looked whole. His brain could be scrambled, for all Hondo knew, but he pulled his ziplock out of his cargo pack and put the body into stasis, then triggered the Come Find Me.

Closer to the center of the defense, Hondo and Ben had better luck. This was where the Malakh-equipped host had fought and died. It took a few minutes to figure out the Malakh's emergency molt, but between the two of them, they managed to extract 23 bodies. Laying them in a row, Hondo searched for Brotherhood stasis packs. He was able to scrounge up 18 working packs, which were activated with the exact same controls as the Federation ziplocks.

"Thank heaven for standardization," he muttered.

He triaged the bodies by his impression of the severity of the wounds that had killed them, then put the best—if any of them could be considered "best"—into stasis. Ben gave up his ziplock, which was a Federation unit built for the larger Klethos, and the 19th body went into that.

The recall came just as they were ziplocking the last one. Ben looked at him, waiting for him to make a decision, but Hondo was not about to leave. He acknowledged the recall, then kept searching.

Over the next two hours, they found 34 more bodies and managed to discover a pack with 50 Brotherhood ziplocks. After taking care of the four that hadn't been previously put into stasis, that meant they had 12 ziplocks left. The problem was that they couldn't find anyone to put in them.

Hondo stopped and scanned the battlefield. He was sure there were more somewhat-whole bodies out there, but he just couldn't find them. Time was getting short. An hour or so after death, every minute that followed decreased the chance for a successful resurrection. The battle had ended six hours ago. Mind-loss would be pretty far advanced by now.

Still, he had to look. He hadn't hit the far flank yet, so he stepped off, checking each fighting hole and piece of cover. He found two ravaged torsos and one badly damaged body, probably too damaged for a resurrection, but with extra ziplocks, it was no harm, no foul.

He walked up to the second-to-last fighting hole and peered in. There was a blackened body at the bottom of the hole, but it looked intact. Hondo called for Ben to come help, and as he started to slide into the hole, he saw two white eyes staring out of the soot-covered face.

"Ben, Ben! This guys' alive!" he shouted.

"Are you OK?" he asked, sliding to kneel beside the man.

Shit, McKeever! No, he's not OK.

The Brotherhood soldier didn't answer, but just stared at him. Hondo reached forward and touched the man's neck. His pulse was reedy and weak, but at least it was there.

Ben reached the hole and slid in as well. He reached for the man's legs to lift him out.

"Wait, we don't know if it's safe to move him!"

The Klethos, for all their technological superiority in so many areas, seemed to lag behind humans when it came to medical care. For example, they didn't have ziplocks nor resurrection. Moving the soldier without assessing him could do more harm than good.

Hondo wasn't a corpsman, though, so he pulled up the basic field medical procedures on his PA and started going through the checklist. The soldier said nothing during the process, only grunting once when Hondo tried to straighten one of his legs.

"I can't tell exactly what's wrong with him," he told Ben.

"He's been wounded by the Grubs," Ben said, the master of the obvious.

Hondo rolled his eyes, then asked once again, "Can you understand me?"

The man twitched his eye. Hondo wasn't sure if that was a conscious movement, so he said, "If you can understand me, blink your eye again."

This time, he was sure the man had twitched.

So, he's conscious. But for how long?

Hondo wasn't an expert, but he thought the man had faded even during the short time he'd been there.

A living person was not generally put into stasis. There was a 2% failure rate for bringing people out of stasis, but that was counterweighed by the fact that a wounded person put into stasis had a greater chance of being brought out than a KIA had of being brought back and resurrected. If this man was going to die anyway, then his chances of survival were better if he got ziplocked now. That wasn't a decision that Hondo felt he could make, however.

He leaned forward and looked the man in the eye. "I think you're in bad shape. You've been burnt at a minimum, and there's nerve damage. I think your best chance is to be ziplocked—I mean, put into stasis." He didn't know if the Brotherhood used the same slang as the Marines. "I've got a stasis pack here, and I can put you in it, but that's your call."

The man just stared at him, unable to speak.

"OK, look. I think this is the best thing for you, but you have to OK it. If you agree, blink again."

It took a few moments, but the eyelid twitched once more.

"OK, Ben," he said, straightening up. "Let's get him out of this hole so we can ziplock him."

"I tried to get him out twenty minutes ago before you stopped me," Ben said.

Hondo ignored the comment, then moved to the man's head, sliding his arms under the wounded soldier's.

"You're going to be OK, I promise you," Hondo said, and then to Ben, "On three. One . . . two . . . three!"

The man grunted louder as they got him up and out of the hole, a cloud of stench rising up and making Hondo gag. Flesh sloughed off his right arm, exposing white, shiny bone.

"Hurry up," Hondo shouted to Ben. "Give me a ziplock."

The man had to be in pain, and Hondo wanted to stop that. It still took two minutes to maneuver the body into the bag, and tears rolled down the man's otherwise expressionless face.

"I'm sorry, I'm sorry. Just a few moments longer."

Ben put a handful of flesh into the bag as Hondo was sealing it.

"They can't use that!" he snapped as he closed the bag.

He gave it a quick check, then activated the stasis. Beneath the clear faceshield, he watched the panic set in as the field began to slow down the atoms that made up the soldier's body. Then the eyes faded. It was done.

"I never got his name," Hondo said as he entered the data and activated the Come Find Me.

Leaving the body in place, the two teammates searched for another hour, finding no one. Finally, Hondo called a stop to their efforts. It was time to go.

They gathered up the last few ziplocked soldiers and carried them to where they'd laid out the others. The Come Find Me should allow each to be easily found, but there was no use taking chances. Whether the bodies were recovered tomorrow or in ten years, Hondo wanted to make it as easy as possible for the recovery team.

He considered carrying the last soldier to their podsuits, but he knew that wouldn't work. He'd have to leave some of the equipment behind to manage that, even if it could be done. If it were a matter of life-and-death, he'd unhesitatingly do it, but in stasis, time was not of the essence, and he'd probably be better off if a ship-of-the-line, with a full medical sickbay, facilitated the recovery.

Human and Klethos climbed back to their hide where Hondo strapped on his kinesthesis frame. They loaded the instruments for the long hike to their podsuits.

Hondo took a moment to look back over the valley. So many had died there, all to get the data that had been uplinked. He hoped it was all worth it.

"Let's go home, Ben," he said as he turned away and stepped off.

ITZUKO-2

Chapter 12
Hondo

> *Staff Sergeant McKeever,*
>
> *Please excuse the unofficial nature of this message, but I wanted to personally thank you and your teammate for your actions on Designated Planet D2. Although my government has received no official word on your actions, we knew that someone had put 58 of our soldiers in stasis and initiated a CASEVAC, preserving their bodies until our forces could recover them. Without that action, none of the fallen could have been saved. As it is, 49 have been resurrected and are expected to make full recoveries.*
>
> *The task force command has remained silent on what exactly happened despite our inquiries. However, one of those you saved was AR3 Rystel Fuentes, who was conscious when you put him into stasis. He reported that a Federation Marine and a Klethos warrior found him and saved his life. Once we knew that, it was not difficult to track you down.*
>
> *The Brotherhood of Man suffered grievous losses in the battles on D2, and our hearts are heavy. However, we have joy that 49 of our soldiers have been returned to their families. We owe that to you.*

The UAM does not want to acknowledge your actions, but my government cannot ignore what you did for us, so from this moment forward, you've been designated a Friend of the Brotherhood of Man. This will accord you full rights of citizenship, should you ever step on a Brotherhood planet.

On a personal note, should you ever have the opportunity, I'd like to invite you to come to Saint Barnabas as an honored guest. I am sure we will have 49 families who would love to meet you, as would I.

Judah III
First Brother

"Does yours say the same thing?" Hondo asked Ben as he looked up from his PA.

"As I have not read yours, I cannot answer that, but it was complimentary."

Hondo grabbed Ben's PA and scanned his message. There were a few words changed—enough to see that the first brother (or some lackey) hadn't just copied and pasted the same letter—but the basic messages were the same. They'd found out that it was Ben and him that had put their soldiers into stasis, and the first brother himself had sent a simple message on the commercial net to both of them.

"Not bad for a demon, there, buddy," Hondo said.

"Yes, I would surmise that I am the first 'demon' to be so honored," Ben replied.

Hondo thought the entire incident was funny, in a sad way. He and Ben had been reprimanded for taking the time to ziplock the soldiers. Some civilian, of all people, had lectured them on the importance of their mission, and that without the data gathered, all the deaths would have been wasted.

The man didn't understand military culture, that was obvious. You simply did not abandon your dead and wounded. Those soldiers may have been Brotherhood, and Hondo was not a fan of them, but they were on the same side now. He could not have simply walked off and let them rot in the field.

Hondo mentioned that the data had already been uplinked, and the man mumbled something about a "forensic wash" of the instruments which had to be done, and that the two of them had jeopardized that.

"But you got it all back, so why are you complaining?" Hondo had asked, getting fed up with what was happening.

"Staff Sergeant, that's enough," commanded Lieutenant Colonel Ghorbani, a Federation Marine and the executive officer of the Interrecon Regiment.

Hondo looked at the colonel in surprise. He, of all people, should have known that a Marine could not abandon others on the battlefield.

"Dr. Boutros, let me handle it from here, if you don't mind," the colonel told the civilian.

The man hesitated, and Hondo knew he wanted to say more, but finally, he nodded and left.

"You were given orders to leave, and you took it upon yourself to disobey those orders."

"But sir—"

"I don't want to hear it. You were given orders. So, consider yourself admonished."

Admonished? What the heck does that actually mean? Hondo had wondered.

"This will be part of both of your temporary service records."

"But those won't follow us . . ." Hondo started to say, when he realized what that meant.

The CO had been ordered to take action by people higher up the food chain, almost certainly civilians. As a Marine, the XO was told to administer the punishment—a punishment that meant absolutely nothing. Just as neither of them had received a medal for snatching the shitpod, this so-called admonishment wouldn't follow Hondo when he was eventually transferred. And that transfer was not going to happen anytime soon, as he had half-feared.

The UAM had squawked, the military arm had acted, and nothing had come of it. Now, two days later, both Hondo and Ben had received a personal message from the freaking first brother of the Brotherhood with an invitation to visit Saint Barnabas, no less.

He looked back down at his PA. Rystel Fuentes. He'd wondered about the man's name at the time, and now he knew. And he felt a strong desire to meet him again.

There was no way he'd be allowed to go to Saint Barnabas and meet the first brother now, and probably not even after he transferred, but right then and there, he promised himself that he'd do it some day.

And he'd take Ben with him.

GOLDEN HAPPINESS STATION

Chapter 13
Skylar

The Dictymorph stood still on the other side of the glass. Sky had to shake off the feeling that the thing was watching the gathered scientists. All in all, it gave her the creeps. Once she'd tasted death as a Dictymorph reached out for her, it was embedded in her very being, and despite her attempt to remain above it all, she could feel the tremors in her soul.

"Commence," she said, trying unsuccessfully to keep her voice centered.

One of the junior staff pushed a green button on a control box that was mounted on the wall, and everyone leaned forward slightly, as if a few centimeters would really help them see better.

A door on the left side of the chamber opened, and Dr. Willis Jain and three technicians in white enviro suits pushed a gurney on which their D-Cell lay. Sky half-expected the Dictymorph to erupt in a storm of light tendrils and cut the Willis and the technicians down.

Come on, Sky. It's a freaking simulacrum, not the real thing!

It may have been an animated model, as accurate as humans could possibly make it, but it was not the real thing. Costing as much as a Navy frigate, the Dictymorph mimicked the actual creature in as much detail as possible. The skin, in particular, was as close to the real thing as they could manage. It had the same cellular structure, and it was heated to the same temperature as a real Dictymorph. It reflected light on the same wavelengths, and its smell was a direct match according to their Support Vector Chronometer. The simulacrum might not have deadly light tendrils with which to kill, but her subconscious kept telling her that was a living Dictymorph in there.

She couldn't quite suppress a shudder as Dr. Jain led his team to the rear of the Dictymorph. They placed the gurney alongside it, then stepped back.

Nothing happened.

Ten minutes later, Dr. Julia Hyperama, who was running the test, signaled Jain to move to Phase 2. Sky wasn't surprised. While the recordings of the D-Cells "in the wild" had shown them to be mobile, this one had shown no inclination to move since its arrival. Phase 1 was a test to see if being in the vicinity of a Dictymorph would spur it into action.

That assumed, however, that their simulacrum would "fool" the mindless D-Cell, and that was a dangerous assumption to make.

The next step was to see if the D-Cell would attach itself if it was physically placed on their Dictymorph. Jain motioned to his team, and they moved forward with antistatic gloves, ready to lift it.

"Let's see if the S-Po likes this," someone said quietly behind her.

Sky turned around and glared, trying to see who said that. This "S-Po" was a new term, and Sky found it slightly ridiculous. The accepted terminology for the Dictymorph sample was "D-Cell," and as scientists, they had to stick with standard terminology to prevent misunderstandings.

No one caught her eye, so she slowly turned back to observe the second of nine different tests to see if they could get the D-Cell to connected with their Dictymorph.

A real Dictymorph could change its shape at will, and even in the default Grub-like shape, they had significant variance between each other, so it wasn't surprising that the recordings did not show an exact placement of the D-Cells. They were generally towards the back, which made sense. That would help to protect the cells from an enemy at its front.

Jain had been instructed to place the D-Cell in the general location they'd observed on actual Dictymorphs, so his four-man team lifted the D-Cell, shuffle-stepped over, and placed it on the Dictymorph . . . and it promptly slid off to the floor.

"Shit," Olaf Kristenov said from two seats down. "Pick it up!"

"It's fine," Sister Keiko told him. "It's pretty impervious to damage."

"And we know that how?"

Dr. Kristenov did not get along with the mother superior. He did not think her team of monks had the same mental capacity as the rest of them. Sky thought his dislike was related to his opinions on religion, but she never voiced that to him. He was brilliant in his own right, and as long has he didn't impede their progress, Sky was not going to jump into that mess.

"Try again, this time higher on the simulacrum," Julia ordered through the speaker system.

Jain nodded, and the four picked up the D-Cell again, this time holding it with outstretched arms as they placed it on the Dictymorph.

Bring in a lifter of some sort, Sky subvocalized into her PA.

It was ridiculous that they had four people standing on tip-toes to try and place the D-Cell.

This time, the D-Cell stayed in place. Sky turned to look at Heinkle Schmitz, the tech on the display, but he caught her eyes and shook his head. The D-Cell was just sitting there, held in place by friction and gravity.

She checked the time. After ten minutes, they would move to the next phase, and then the next and the next after that until they learned how the cell attached itself. That is, if they ever learned. The D-Cell could be damaged, or the Dictymorph might not be a good enough copy. They could set everything up correctly, yet no melding would occur because of other factors.

This one isn't happening, Sky told herself as she checked her PA.

She had a long queue of messages, so she took advantage of the time to start answering them.

She'd responded to two of them when someone shouted out, "Look at the S-Po."

There were murmurs from around her as she looked up. She didn't notice anything different about the D-Cell, but others had.

Several were now standing. Sky glanced at Heinkle on the display, and he was sitting tall in his seat, his body tense.

After a long five seconds, he turned around and announced to the room, "We have a connection."

Sky couldn't just sit there. She rushed to the display, looking at the readouts.

"Right here, ma'am. That's a good connection. The molecules have locked," he said.

The underside skin of the D-Cell had an interesting pattern of high and low spots at the microscopic level. Malcolm Orrisy had said they reminded him of dovetail joints used in woodworking. Sky had never examined real wood furniture, but she understood the concept, and Orrisy's observations seemed sound. The Dictymorphs could easily mold their skin into dovetail joints as well, and so the back portion of the simulacrum was manufactured with the joints and slots already formed.

Sky thought the idea was possible, but she hadn't placed that much weight into the idea that those alone would trigger a connection. It looked like she was wrong.

"And now we have power!" Heinkle shouted, his voice filled with excitement.

Sky hadn't needed him to tell her that. She'd seen the display light up, indicating a flow of energy from the D-Cell into the half-empty batteries installed inside the simulacrum.

Cheers erupted in the room. The technology that she'd just witnessed bordered on the fantastic. The wizards at Lucas-Samsung had managed not only to build a life-sized, realistic-looking Dictymorph, but they'd managed to fool a D-Cell into thinking it was the real thing.

"Great job, Dr. Ybarra," Kristenov said, slapping her on the back. "We did it."

"Yes, great job, everyone," Sky said, but with a lot less enthusiasm.

They'd managed to get the D-Cell to meld with the simulacrum, but that was only the first part of the battle. They'd done this test to see how the D-Cell attached to the Dictymorph. Now came the real part of the project.

They had to figure out how to take it off.

ITZUKO-2

Chapter 14
Hondo

"How about that one?" Hondo asked.

Byron shrugged and said, "As long as they've got a pint, I don't care where we drink."

AR6 Taster Knowles looked at their three Klethos teammates, but when they didn't say anything, he nodded.

Maryanne's was just one more over-priced dive. It looked like an old family bar, but Hondo knew it was part of the Itzuko corporate holdings. Itzuko mined only a small portion of the planet, then received huge amounts of rent from the Federation for the Marines, and now even more from the UAM for the lease of land that they had never intended to use in the first place. Even after receiving all that free credit, they were still determined to wring every centicredit they could from the Marines and visiting forces.

It didn't matter much to Hondo, however. Interrecon was stuck far out in the boonies, out of the way of prying eyes, and their own E-Club was rather lacking in social amenities. The trip to Camp Ceasare for weapons fitting gave the three friends a chance to hit the ville for an evening, and like all good soldiers, they weren't going to let that opportunity to go to waste.

They'd been surprised when their Klethos teammates had followed them off-base as if it was assumed that they'd all go out together. The Klethos didn't drink alcohol—and thought it was strange that humans did. They did love salty foods, however, so their little E-Club had long been out of peanuts and assorted bar snacks. Hondo wasn't sure if the Klethos would enjoy hanging out in a bar or not—peanuts notwithstanding—but Ben was his teammate, and if he, Horace, and Big Tom wanted to come, then so be it.

Hondo pushed open the doors to the place. Ten Marines, all in their civilian gear, were inside the dimly-lit bar. Two were playing Crake—one had an intricate cue, complete with inlaid mother-of-pearl.

Probably fake, Hondo told himself as he walked up to the bar.

The Marines were not recruits, but they weren't old salts, either, and some of the higher-end crake cues could sell for six month's salary for a non-rate.

Itzuko was primarily an armor training planet. Federation and allied treadheads loved the wide-open—and empty—spaces to play their war games. So far, tankers had a very limited role in fighting the Grubs. Like aircraft, they were quickly taken out of action. So, they trained on planets like the Itch for yesterday's wars, dreaming of becoming relevant again. The Marines had that treadhead look about them—a little shorter than average, but with broad shoulders. They had on clean civvies, but Hondo could still conjure up the grease and dirt of the tank dock under their fingernails. They all looked up when the three humans walked in, and Hondo could see that just as he knew they were treadheads, they knew the three of them were something different—something probably better left alone. The guy with the fancy cue made a deliberate turn back toward the table, ignoring them.

Then the three Klethos pushed their way into the bar, stopping to look around in what Hondo now recognized as open curiosity. All talking ceased.

"May I help you, sir?" the autotender asked, a gorgeous model with too large breasts.

Hondo's eyes automatically drifted down the large expanse of cleavage before he jerked his head back up.

Come on, McKeever. You haven't been in the bush for that long.

Autotenders like these were made to read pupil dilation, respiration, and other physical signs, and this one reacted as programmed, leaning forward and looking with adoring eyes at his face.

"What do you have on tap?" Hondo asked, his face getting red.

He hoped no one had noticed him ogling its plastitits.

"O'Doul's, Harrison, Blue Lodge, Budweiser, OB—"

"Give me an OB," Hondo said, stopping the litany.

He was surprised that this dive had so many beers on draft. Then again, it wasn't really a dive, just a facade of one, with all the corporate economies of scale behind it.

"And send us a bowl of peanuts and pretzels," he said, looking back at the three Klethos. "Better make that two big bowls of each."

"Certainly, sir."

She . . . it . . . poured him a stein, stopping a microsecond before the foam would have spilled over the rim. Itzuko wouldn't allow any waste here. Hondo took the stein and the first bowl of peanuts to an empty table, then motioned for the three Klethos to sit while the other two got their drinks.

He was aware of every eye in the place staring at them. Not that he blamed them. As tankers, this might be the first time any of them had seen an actual Klethos close up.

Klethos weren't really designed to sit—particularly not in chairs that hadn't made for them—so after grabbing handfuls of peanuts, they wandered around the bar, looking just as intensely at the hanging lamps as the faux combat pics on the walls.

"Look at them," Taster said after he downed his second stein in a single long swallow. "Like cats, curious about everything."

"They don't got no nine lives, though," Byron added. "Unfortunately."

All three raised their glasses and clinked them together; a toast to fallen comrades. Interrecon had started with 24 teams: 24 humans and 24 Klethos. Now, less than a year later, there were only 13 of the original humans and nine Klethos left. A Klethos, even a male Klethos, was still stronger and more robust than any human, and yet more of them had been killed. Hondo thought it was because they weren't, well, as *careful* as their human teammates.

That was why he hounded Ben in the field, micromanaging him as he wouldn't another Marine. He'd gotten close to Ben, and he didn't want to lose his friend.

At the moment, Ben seemed fascinated by the crake game. The Marine with the fancy cue was pretty good, imparting just enough spin to fly the balls through the pillions but not careen out of control. The two Marines playing were obviously aware of him, but just as obviously ignoring him.

After one shot by the second Marine, when the key ball settled back down to the felt, Ben reached out with his left upper hand and gently touched it.

"Oh, shit," Hondo said, jumping to his feet.

"Hey, you can't do that!" the Marine yelled, pushing his chest into the larger Klethos, who took a step back.

"Look at that," the first Marine said, and several others started forward to the table. "She's a-scared, and she's not so big, not like they tell us."

They don't know our Klethos are males, he realized. *Doesn't matter. I've got to put a stop to this.*

"Stand down, Marines," Hondo said, putting all his drill instructor rasp into his voice.

He was obviously older than any of the Marines, so they should have known that he was senior to them all.

Maybe he'd been too long outside of the real Corps, because Fancy-Cue simply sneered at him and said, "So, who's the Kluck lover here?"

"This *Kluck-lover* is a staff sergeant, that's who he is."

The Marine stepped back, but then the other, the one who'd chest-bumped Ben and whose breath reeked of booze, said, "I'm calling bullshit. You ain't no fucking Marine, not if you hang out with Klucks."

Byron stepped up beside Hondo and said, "Let's keep it calm, boys."

His accent seemed to astound the drunk Marine, who said, "Lookie here. We got ourselves a Brotherhood coward."

Taster, who'd stepped up on the other side of Hondo, tensed. Byron was a Confederation soldier. Taster was Brotherhood.

Not many Marines liked the Brotherhood. They'd abandoned the alliance, after all, and were only forced back in. Hondo hadn't liked the Brotherhood, either, but Taster was a good guy. More than that, he was a fellow recon warrior. They were brothers-in-arms.

"And what do you have against the Brotherhood?" Byron asked with a taunt in his voice.

Hondo put his arm across Byron's chest. They didn't need to start anything. He knew from the bottom of his military heart that the three of them were more than a match for any of the treadheads, even as big as some of them were, but there were eight of them, and they'd promised the major that they'd keep a low profile.

"What do I have against you? You're fucking cowards, that's what I have against you."

Like a flash, Taster stepped forward, grabbed the drunk's cue, and smashed it over his knee. The cue was made from some alloy, and it bent in two.

"I'll show you cowards, you bloody piece of shit!"

"Stop it!" Hondo shouted, but he knew it was too late.

He ducked a swing from Fancy-Cue, feeling the mother-of-pearl beauty whiz just past his chin. There was a crash beside him—whether it was Byron dishing it out or taking it in, he couldn't take the time to see. Fancy-Cue was swinging again. Hondo ducked beneath the swing, and with the Marine now off-balance and exposed, Hondo rose with a wicked shot to the Marine's side.

Fancy-Cue collapsed to one knee, his mouth open as he gasped for air, the cue falling to the ground and rolling away. Hondo jumped forward to grab it and stood, ready to use it as a weapon.

Byron was being held by one of the Marines while another was pounding on him. He was roaring like a buffalo, but he couldn't shake the one holding him. On top of the crake table, Taster had the drunk Marine on his back and was pounding him, as another Marine was punching him in the lower back. Taster didn't seem to notice, but he couldn't take that kind of punishment forever.

Hondo stepped forward, cue ready to swing when something crashed against his head, stunning him. He fell to his knees as beer drenched him. One of the bastards had cold-cocked him with a stein, and now he was coming to finish him off. Hondo tried to shake it off and get to his feet, but he knew he was toast.

So did his opponent, a huge Marine with muscles on his muscles. He smiled as he raised a fist to knock Hondo back down . . . and suddenly, he was jerked off his feet. Ben had waded in and was holding the big Marine in the air while the man kicked his feet and screamed.

"Don't kill him, Ben," Hondo managed to croak out.

Ben almost nonchalantly threw the Marine over the crake table, where he hit hard and lay still. Hondo managed to get to his feet, ready to continue, but the fight was over. With three down by the human threesome, the three Klethos had made short work of the rest. Two weren't moving, and the rest were barely able to crawl away.

Hondo staggered up to Fancy -Cue, who was still in pain and on his knees.

"Please be advised that I have called for the police," the autotender said.

Hell, she's even sexy when she's saying she's called the cops.

Something warmer than beer was dripping down his neck, and Hondo reached up, bringing back down a hand red with blood. He looked at Fancy -Cue, who looked back up at him with sullen and defeated eyes.

"I am a staff sergeant, Marine. Striking a staff non-commissioned officer is assault. Did you know that?"

If his expression was any indication, then yes, he did know that.

"Luckily, this was all a wrestling match. Don't you agree?" he asked, raising his voice so that all of them could hear.

The slightest bit of hope appeared in the Marine's eyes.

"It might have gotten a little out-of-hand, but you know, Marines are Marines. We work hard, and we play hard. Luckily, this was just between us humans. The Klethos were not involved."

"Bullshit. That fucking Kluck about tore off my arm," one of the other Marines shouted out before Fancy-Cue cut her off.

"Zip it, Carrie. The Klucks were not involved."

"But—"

"I said zip it."

"I see you understand," Hondo said.

"And after losing our friendly wager, you're picking up our tab, isn't that right?"

"Yes, sir."

"Oh, I'm not a sir. I work for a living. I told, you, I'm a staff sergeant."

Hondo held out the cue, looking at it. It really was beautiful, and the more he looked at it, the more he thought it might actually be genuine. And he was royally pissed that the bastard had tried to brain him with it.

"This sure is nice. Having something like this in a fight, well, the chances of it getting broken . . ." he said, holding it up like he was going to smash the table with it.

The Marine started to get up, a protest forming on his lips.

"Now, now, now, we have to learn our lesson, right?"

A look of resignation came over his face, and he said, "Yes, Staff Sergeant."

"So, remember that next time. This is not a weapon to use on fellow Marines," Hondo said, placing it undamaged on the crake table.

"Come on, let's go before the cops get here," he said to the other five.

"The bill?" Byron asked.

"Our friends here have offered to pay. We don't need to leave a credit trace of our being here."

The Klethos were still wide-eyed, just looking around, as the three humans pushed and pulled them out of the bar. They got outside and turned down an alley just as the first police hover arrived on the scene.

Hondo let out a huge sigh of relief. They'd barely dodged that bullet.

"That was fun," Ben said, as the hugged the wall of the building to stay out of sight of the cops. "Can we do it again?"

GOLDEN HAPPINESS STATION

Chapter 15
Skylar

Sky watched closely as the robot trundled forward, the prototype firmly in its graspers. This was the third prototype, based on Orange Team's work. The first two had failed, having no effect on the S-Po . . .

D-Cell, she reminded herself.

They had no effect on the *D-Cell.* Orange Team had decided to go with a different approach. They had developed a disrupter, which they thought could sever the bond between D-Cell and Dictymorph. The logic was that if they took out the battery, and a hover couldn't hover, a PA couldn't turn on.

The D-Cell itself almost assuredly didn't give a Dictymorph different capabilities. It just enabled them to withstand human weapons longer. The pulse neutralizers, what the Marines called "grappling hooks," still worked, but it would take more of them and a longer span of time to kill a Dictymorph. All weapons should still work; it would just take them longer, more time in which more humans and Klethos would die.

If a simple weapon could be developed that would detach the D-Cell, then that would be a huge step forward. The Rube Goldberg contraption in the robot's grasper was their first attempt at that.

"Do it," Dr. Harry O'Shaw said, nodding at Lori Godspeed, one of his team members.

Harry was the Orange Team leader, and he looked as dense as a rock with his slack expression and dead eyes. However, that look hid a sharp mind that could worry out the answers to any question. Sky was glad to have him on the team.

Lori punched in the command, and the robot fired the prototype while thousands of measurements were taken. Sky ignored the data—studying it would come later. She wanted to see the D-Cell detach.

After ten seconds, Harry stopped the process. The D-Cell was still clinging to the Dictymorph simulacrum, and a quick look told her that it was also still providing power.

Sky felt a huge letdown. This wasn't the first failure, and it wouldn't be the last, but she'd had high hopes for Harry's weapon. He was now huddled in heated discussion with his team over the major bank of displays as they tried to figure out what had happened.

"I'm going back to my office," she told Sister Keiko.

"I'll walk you back. I need to get back to my team, too," the mother superior said.

The two women stood and started to leave, but just as they reached the door, she heard Harry say, "Let's go to two-eighty and try the F-phase, then run it again. I want to see how that affects the cohesion factor."

Sky stopped and turned back. She wasn't going to get her hopes up, but she could afford a few more minutes. Leaning against one of the seats in the back row, she watched as Lori put in the new parameters. When Harry nodded, she sent the robot the command to fire.

As before, there wasn't anything much to see from the D-Cell itself. The key was the data streaming in, and after only ten seconds, Morgan Chan excitedly pointed at one of the readouts. Immediately the rest of the team crowded around.

"What's going on?" Sky asked.

She was just about to go join them down at the front when the mother superior grabbed her arm and said, "Look!"

The D-Cell was *wrinkling*—that was probably the best way to describe it. Sky watched in fascination as the surface bunched up. A very visible wave crossed its body. A second wave followed, and suddenly, it detached and slipped to the floor.

There was a stunned silence, and then a cheer filled the observation room. Harry's entire team rushed to the glass to see.

Sky started around the row of seats to join them when the room exploded into heat and light, and Sky's world went black.

Chapter 16
Sky

Keyshon sat at the foot of her bed, bent at the waist, head cradled in his hands. He'd just briefed her on what had happened, and Sky needed time to process it.

The explosion of the D-Cell had not been large, but in the confined space of the testing and observation rooms, the effect had been severe. The entire Orange Team had been killed outright, as had three people who'd been sitting in the first two rows. Six people had been seriously hurt, and another twelve—including Sister Keiko and Sky—had needed medical treatment.

Sky and the other eleven would be up and about within a day or two, but the rest had already been evacuated off the station. Some—perhaps even most—would have successful resurrections, but all would be in regen for upwards of a year or more. They would not be returning to *Golden Happiness*.

Ironic name, now, she thought.

As cold as it might seem, the people could be replaced, but not the D-Cell. It was gone. They'd recovered the organic debris, of course, but now humanity only had the one on Taterville. All research on that specimen had been put on hold until they could figure out what happened.

The Dictymorph simulacrum had also been heavily damaged, and one of the station admin bureaucrats had already lectured Sky about that, even before the docs had let Keyshon in to see her. His concern about the cost seemed to overshadow any thought of the dead personnel.

Sky had expected to find out that she'd been relieved of her duty. When pressed, Keyshon had admitted to her that many higher up the chain had wanted that, but the Federation had stood firm. She'd asked Keyshon if that was because the chairman trusted her leadership or if it was because of the politics of the situation, of not wanting the Federation to shoulder any of the blame. Her assistant hadn't answered in words, but his blush had been answer enough.

Sky was still in a state of shock, and she knew medications were coursing through her body, fed in micro-doses by nanos. That dulled the pain, but she couldn't afford that. She was still in charge, and they had to move forward.

Reaching up, she dialed back the meds to zero. Within ten seconds, her brain started to clear up—along with a wave of despair that caused her to gasp. Keyshon looked up, concern on his face.

"I'm OK," she said, holding up her palm. "I just need a sec."

She took several deep breaths. Sky was not a Marine commander, nor the commanding officer of a naval ship. She'd been in danger herself before, but she'd never been in the position to lose subordinates. Not just subordinates—that sounded too removed. These were colleagues, even her friends. And she had been in charge of them, in charge of the research. She could have—should have—stepped in to make sure the working environment was safe.

She'd failed.

But now, she had to push forward. Men and women—and Klethos—were dying trying to hold back the Dictymorph tsunami that was sweeping through the galaxy.

"Tell Purple Team to drop their synchronicity projector. I want them to take the prototype and give me ten field units, ready to go."

"Uh . . . which prototype?" Keyshon asked.

"Which one do you think? Orange Team's."

"But—"

"But nothing. It detached the D-Cell."

"Yes, ma'am. I'll let Dr. Jain know."

"They've got five days."

Keyshon raised his eyebrows at that, but he didn't respond.

"What are you waiting for?" she asked, after ten long seconds.

Keyshon hurried off, leaving Sky in her bed. Sky had started to feel comfortable in her position as a manager, but this had broken that. Once again, she felt like an imposter, someone out of her league.   But this was on her shoulders now, and until she was yanked out of the billet, she'd do the best she could.

Rushing through a field prototype might be hasty given the normal process, but they didn't have the time for that.   The lab prototype had managed to detach the D-Cell, no matter what had happened after that.   But it had detached it from a simulacrum, not an actual Dictymorph.   Before they could proceed, they had to find out how the weapon would work on the actual target.

It was time for a field test.

DESIGNATED PLANET D39

Chapter 17
Hondo

"A fucking field test. I can't believe we're running a field test," Taster said.

"It's just another mission," Byron said. "Why d'ya have your panties in a twist?"

"Our mission is to observe, Byron, not test untried weapons."

"We are observing. What do you think we're humping?"

"We" was a generous term. The three Klethos were doing the heavy lifting of the instruments. The three humans were carrying the weapons prototypes along, with the normal combat load of weapons, food, and supplies.

Hondo understood Taster's unhappiness, though. He felt uneasy as well. D39 had been a terrible defeat for the Human/Klethos task force. Over 40,000 humans—mostly Confederation soldiers, New Budapest Rangers, and Federation Marines, and 6,000 Klethos—had been either killed or forced to withdraw. The Grubs had simply been too powerful, their shitpods provided too many extra energy reserves. There were still an estimated 800 humans on the planet, cut off during the confusion of evacuation. Those 800 were the six Interrecon fighters' cover. With the survivors scattered, the theory was they would make it more difficult for the Grubs to track down three humans and three Klethos.

Hondo knew that every day delayed meant more of the survivors would be killed, and that filled him with a sense of guilt. It wasn't logical. He didn't write the op plan. He still felt the guilt, however.

And now, they'd been chasing ghosts for seven days. As big as Grubs were, he'd have thought it would have been easy to find a target and test the weapons. Yet the only Grub they'd spotted was three days ago, and that one didn't have the shitpod battery pack.

Hondo wondered if they'd even find one. Taking the analogy to the Marines, PICS Marines wouldn't stay in their combat suits 24/7 when major hostilities were over. The PICS would be sent in for maintenance and reload, while the Marines got some downtime. For all he knew, the Grubs were the same. Maybe the shitpods messed them up, and they had to take them off. He knew the Grubs weren't human, and he couldn't transfer human traits onto them. Still, it made sense in a way.

At the moment, the six of them were moving toward a known concentration of Grubs. Comms were spotty, for reasons no one understood, but enough information had made it through for them to locate the Grubs. They'd been on the march now for about eight hours and had another one to go. Hondo just hoped that this wasn't a wild goose chase. He wanted to get the mission done and get off the planet. He wasn't superstitious per se, but a lot of people had died here, so if he did believe in ghosts and tortured spirits . . .

Hell, McKeever. Snap out of it. There's no such thing as ghosts. You're on point, so keep your mind on business.

Hondo fingered the trigger on his M77, the sonic projector. The basic weapon didn't look much different than the one PFC Uriah Joseph had used back on Destiny, but the effectiveness had been much improved. At under 200 meters, it could stop a Grub cold within 20 seconds. If the reports were true, however, if a Grub had a shitpod attached, it might take upwards of a minute. That was a long, long time to keep a Grub under fire and expect to survive, especially with only the cerrostrand shielding for protection.

Behind him, Taster carried the M96. He had only 12 of the 46mm rounds. That wasn't enough, but he had emptied the magazine bunker while they awaited the next shipment. Walking point, he wished he had the M96. They may be limited in rounds, but one of them *could* put down a Grub, even if three or four were more likely to be needed.

They'd been climbing a gentle slope for about a klick before it got steep. Hondo looked back to Taster, who was the team leader for the mission. They could go around or climb. Taster pulled down his display and studied the topo for a moment before he pointed up. They were going to climb.

It took an hour, but they reached the top, a plateau at least 400 meters across. It gave a pretty good view of the surrounding terrain. They should be better able to spot the Grubs from up there, and it might be a good location for all the instrumentation.

"Hondo, you and Ben take a look to the north and see what you can. Byron, you and Horace do the same to the east. Meet us back here in say . . . say an hour."

"Roger that," Hondo said.

Ben dropped his load, and the two moved quickly through the scraggly scrub to the edge of the plateau. Hondo got on his belly and glassed the terrain below them. He spotted two humans about three klicks away, cautiously walking along a tree line, but no Grubs. With ten minutes left, he and Ben returned.

Byron was waiting, but without Horace.

"Saw four Grubs . . ." he said, pausing for dramatic effect, ". . . with shitpods. I left Horace there to keep an eye on them."

"No shit?"

"No shit. Here comes Taster and Big Tom. This is it."

A minute later, the last two arrived, and Bryon briefed the team leader. Taster agreed, and they carried the instruments to the edge of the plateau, the three humans splitting up Horace's load. Down below, about two klicks away, four Grubs slowly moved across an open field. Hondo looked back up to the north. The two humans he'd seen were about five clicks away from the Grubs. That was within the range of the Grub's light tendrils. There wasn't much he could do about it now, though. He didn't have comms, so he'd have to trust them to keep out of the way.

Taster took a long moment to glass the Grubs before he lowered his binos and said, "Looks like this is it. We all know our places, right?"

"Roger that," Hondo and Byron said in unison.

Hondo and Ben went through the upcheck on their two prototypes. These were not field-ready weapons. They barely qualified as man-packed weapons, looking more like construction equipment. The trigger was OK for a four-armed Klethos, but the reach was long for a human. Still, it wasn't as if they were there to defeat the Grubs. There were there to see if firing knocked off a shitpod or not, period. If it did—or even if it didn't—it was fire and beat feet out of there.

"We're up," Hondo announced.

"Byron, are you two ready?" Taster asked.

"Give me one," Byron said as he connected the instruments via heavy data cables.

The instruments seemed primitive to Hondo. Data cables, for goodness sake. But he's been assured that the instruments were battle hardened and suitable for rough handling. Hondo hoped so. He didn't want the mission to be a failure due to primitive equipment.

Horace finally gave a four-thumbs-up, something he always seemed to get a kick out of. They were ready.

"OK, Hondo, let's do it."

Leaving Byron and Horace on top, the four descended down the side of the mesa and out towards where they'd seen their targets.

"The Grubs are on the move towards your left," Byron passed on the team net.

Taster pointed a new direction to Ben, who without the equipment load, was now the point. They shifted their direction, moving 900 meters before Taster stopped them. He studied his display for a moment, then pulled Hondo and Ben in.

"We're going to split up now. Me and Big Tom are gonna head here," he said, touching the outside of his display.

Hondo pulled down his monocle, and the point was highlighted. It was a logical position, over the wash that would be his and Ben's avenue of egress.

"See you on the flip side," Hondo said, reaching out to shake Taster's hand.

Taster clamped him on the shoulder and said, "Run your ass off, if it comes down to it. We've got your six."

Big Tom gave Ben a strong kick in the shin, which thudded loud enough to make Hondo wince. He didn't understand the Klethos' propensity to inflict damage upon themselves before a fight, and he'd never seen the female warriors do that to each other, but the males always seemed to do it. Ben kicked Big Tom back, and, as always, Hondo was glad the Klethos didn't see the need to include humans in that little ceremony.

The two teams split, and Hondo and Ben continued slightly to the northeast. After another 600 meters, the local tree analogs thinned out as they approached the open field. Both went prone and low-crawled far enough forward until they spotted first one, then all four Grubs.

"How far do you think they are?" Hondo asked.

"Eight hundred meters," Ben said without hesitation.

Why do I even ask?

The Grubs were probably closer to 400 meters. Klethos didn't seem to be very numbers-conscious. They understood the concept of near and far, but the exact numbers didn't seem to matter much to them. How they could be so technologically advanced in so many areas with such a disregard for numbers was beyond him. The male Klethos, at least, understood that humans were far more anal about numbers, and so they were happy to offer distances, weights, and even time with the least encouragement—just with a complete disregard for reality. Hondo didn't know if Ben was just saying the first figure that came to his head or if he really thought the Grubs were 800 meters away.

To fire the weapons, they'd been told that they should be within 200 meters.

"Why the hell can't they give us stand-off weapons?" Taster had asked when they'd been briefed.

Hondo agreed. It seemed that in today's modern universe, the distance to reach out and touch an enemy was shrinking. First, the Klethos and human gladiators battled with swords. Now, against the Grubs, things were not much better when a pike was still a weapon of choice.

It is what it is. Now, how to close the distance?

Hondo's Ruger sidearm had a simple laser rangefinder, and he was tempted to range the big beasts, but they'd shown that they were able to detect lasers in the past. It would be better to just close the distance until he was sure that they were within range.

The four Grubs were intermittently moving a few meters, stopping, and then moving again. He didn't have a clue as to what they were doing, but that didn't matter.

To their left, a small runoff creased the field. If the Grubs kept moving the way they were, then they would pass close to the far end of the depression. That runoff would give the two their best opportunity as long as the Grubs remained in the open. If they moved back into the trees, then things would get much easier for the two teammates.

Hondo and Ben pulled back and approached the near end of the runoff, using the trees for cover. He stood to check the Grubs once more, then got on his belly for another long, elbow-rubbing, knee-piercing low-crawl. Sweat poured down his neck as he crawled, then found its way into his eyes, making them burn. Hondo kept rubbing them, but his filthy right hand simply pushed the sweat around. He didn't even try to rub his eyes with his left hand—the prosthetic was good for most purposes, but not for a poke in the eye.

About half way across the field, the slight depression flattened out, giving the two of them even less cover. Even prone, he could see the four Grubs, and if he could see *them*, they could see *him*. It didn't surprise him that they didn't react yet, but that didn't mean they wouldn't.

Hondo signaled for Ben to stop. He didn't want to push it, and if the Grubs kept advancing, they'd pass by at maybe 120 meters, well within their parameters.

"Check your weapon. Remember, I'll go with my first setting. If we still need it, you'll go after me on your first setting."

Ben gave him four thumbs-up.

Oh, God, he's taking after Horace now, he thought, slowly shaking his head.

Hondo unslung the prototype and pulled it up so he could see the selector lever. Two pieces of duct tape were attached to the side, one above the other. On one, someone had scribbled "Trial One." On the other was "Trial Two."

That didn't give Hondo a warm-and-fuzzy. "Trial" sounded like a test, which of course this was, but possibly one where they didn't even know if the weapon would fire.

Ben's weapon had "Trial 3" and "Trial 4" written on his two pieces of tape. The science-type who'd briefed them had told them that the different trials were at different settings. If possible, they were to fire all four settings for a minimum of 20 seconds each.

Oh, hell yeah. No problem, Hondo had thought at the time. *I can hold on target while a 12-meter Grub charges me.*

Hondo had asked if he and Ben could fire at the same time, one on Trial 1 and the other on Trial 2. The geek looked at Hondo as if he were a child, and in a very condescending tone said that no, they couldn't do that as it could interfere with the instrumentation.

Hondo had wanted to take the prototype, which he had been holding at the time, and shove it up the guy's asshole—sideways—but he'd managed to withstand following through on the thought. When he'd told Byron, his friend said that he deserved a medal for being able to resist the temptation.

He flipped the ungainly lever back and forth. He didn't think it mattered which one he used first. They would have mentioned that, he figured, but it was probably better to go with number 1, just to be safe.

With the prototype beside him, he looked up. The Grubs still showed no sign of acknowledging their presence. As soon as Hondo fired, however, he knew that would change.

"You ready?" he asked Ben.

Ben let his weapon drop to give him four thumbs-up before picking it back up again.

The prone position was the most stable position from which to fire a weapon. Normally, 150 meters was nothing, but the prototype did not act like a normal weapon. It rattled, and everything seemed loosely held together. He'd considered rising to his knees for a better view, but he thought he'd better stick with the prone.

He sighted down the simple post sight at the tip of the barrel. It was slightly canted to the side where the welder hadn't centered it correctly, but it would have to do. He was firing a multilobe beam, with the main lobe spreading out to more than a meter. He should be able to hit the shitpod.

The first Grub eased into his vision. Hondo waited until he had a sight-picture of the (relatively) small limpet-like shitpod on the Grub's back.

Might as well take this one, he thought as he squeezed the trigger, holding it open.

The weapon let out a high-pitched whine that made his hair stand on end. For a moment, the Grub didn't show any sign of being hit, and Hondo almost pulled back the weapon to make sure it was firing, but suddenly, the Grub started shaking, small light tendrils shooting off it like miniature bolts of lightning.

"Come on, baby, fall off!" he muttered, holding this weapon steady despite the fact that it was heating up.

From the practice shots fired on the Itch, he knew that this was "normal" for this specific weapon, but it was hardly normal for anything else. His nose began to itch as a nasty ozone-smell assaulted him. Another Grub lumbered into view, almost blocking his shot, but he managed to keep it on target for the full 20 seconds.

The shitpod was still attached, and the Grub was looking agitated.

"Ben, go!"

Ben fired, hitting the nearest Grub. It didn't react with the same intensity, but it was obviously pissed as well. The two Grubs seemed to be casting about for the source of the fire, but it was another tendril of light that shot through the air just over their heads. Either the third or fourth Grub had located them.

Hondo counted down the seconds, and as soon as it hit 20, he grabbed Ben and yelled, "Let's get out of here! Keep your head down!"

He flipped up and over himself and started crabbing, ignoring his sore knees and elbows. He felt, more than saw, Ben on his ass. More light tendrils danced over their heads, one actually brushing him. His shielding held, but barely, and that was the lightest of touches.

The farther they low-crawled, the more cover they had. They were reaching safety, but that would only be temporary. The Grubs were coming. He didn't have to look to know that was true.

Hondo reached the trees first. He got behind one trunk, then stood.

"Holy shit, they're close. Hurry, Ben!"

He flipped the lever to Trial 2, hoping to get a shot at the shitpod, but the front of the closest Grub was shielding it. He had to get a side aspect.

"Go to the right and pick yourself a target, then fire," he told Ben before bolting to the left. A light tendril reached for him, but the tree trunks took the brunt of the damage. After running 30 or 40 meters, he stopped and looked. He could just see the edge of the shitpod on the lead Grub.

"That's gotta do," he said aloud as he sighted in and fired. The Grub he'd hit shuddered, contracted slightly into a rounder shape, then elongated again, light shooting off it. Ten meters to Hondo's left, a tree exploded, shards and splinters of wood shooting in all directions. Something hit Hondo on his leg, but his armor hardened, and nothing penetrated.

At twenty seconds—or maybe seventeen, if he was being honest—the Grub turned towards him, and he lost the sight picture on the shitpod. A light tendril shot right at him, blasting the trunk that he'd been taking cover behind. Hondo dropped to the ground and chewed up the dirt with his heels as he scooted backward on his butt to get out of the line of fire. He hit another tree, so he turned belly-down to get behind it.

Trees were exploding all around him, filling the air with wooden shrapnel. Pieces peppered him, even from behind the tree. He grabbed his sonic projector, edged his head around the tree, and a splinter penetrated his cheek all the way into his mouth.

"*Moddurfuh!*" he mumbled, blood filling his mouth.

He reached up with his left hand, clamped it on the end of the wooden shard, and yanked, tearing it out—along with half of his cheek. He activated his personal doc, and it sent coagunanos streaming to the site. There was no way they could repair his cheek, but they could slow the flow of blood to the surrounding tissue.

"*Somofuhbitz!*" he shouted, blood spraying as he whipped around the tree trunk, then fired off a blast at the Grub hovering just outside the treeline. It shuddered, and then responded with multiple light tendrils that reached into the forest to seek him out.

Hondo dove back into cover, and he knew he had to move. His cheek was numbing up nicely, but that was the least of his worries. He got to his knees, took three deep breaths, then bolted back towards Ben.

"*Brek contag*," he passed, his mouth having trouble pronouncing the words, and hoped that his teammate was on the net.

Hondo and Ben may have fired their prototype weapons, but now they had to get out of there, and the plan was to lead the Grubs past Taster and Big Tom's position. Byron had his twelve rounds, and even if the civilian scientists hadn't asked for it, the military side of the house wanted to gather more data on the effectiveness of the rounds against powered-up Grubs. The rounds had been used during the earlier defeat, but with all the civilian instrumentation available to the team, the military R&D folks could siphon off that data as well.

There was a crashing through the underbrush, and Hondo raised his projector before he saw Ben emerge. Hondo didn't say anything, just simply started running with Ben on his ass. Several times, light tendrils reached for them. Hondo felt the numbness of glancing blows several times, and once, Ben fell and rolled on the ground. Hondo stopped and pulled his teammate up, and with two arms around his shoulders, the two of them limped on. Another light tendril creased them just as they dropped into a tiny wash crossing in front of them.

Hondo didn't know where they were or how far away from Taster and Big Tom they were, but they had to keep going. The problem was that he knew there was no way they could outrun four Grubs out in the relatively open ground. They had to go back into the trees along the slopes of the mesa.

He also needed more energy. With a sense of regret, he subvocalized his PD to begin a stim release. Almost immediately, he felt a surge of energy. It was all a facade, of course. His body had no more actual energy. This stim only allowed him to access what energy he did have quicker. He still had nerve damage, and he still had lost blood. And when he hit the end of the rope, he'd collapse, his reserves depleted.

Still, it was the only choice.

The wash had been cut by runoff from the plateau above them, so Hondo got back to his feet and bodily lifted Ben. Together, they pushed to their left, deeper into the trees and the slope. He knew they could be trapping themselves. As they got higher up, where the trees were smaller, they'd be visible to the Grubs below who could take them under fire.

For two minutes, they moved in relative silence, broken only by the sound of their heavy breathing. Hondo felt lightheaded, but otherwise fine as they climbed. He kept looking back, but the trees blocked his view.

They didn't block the rope of light that slammed into the ground five meters to their left.

"Go!" Hondo said, pulling Ben to reach the safety of the plateau, all the time knowing it was a hopeless quest.

And then the sweet, sweet sound of an M96 opened up, with four sharp cracks.

"Taster!" he shouted, at the same time as Ben yelled "Big Tom!"

"Now, move it while we've got covering fire."

The two struggled up the slope as it got steeper, while behind them, the slow, measured cracks of Byron's M96 echoed around them, the report bouncing off the rocks. Hondo counted each shot.

He looked back once, and light tendrils lit up the trees.

At the eleventh round, the two stumbled over the edge and onto the plateau itself. They were safe—for the moment.

If the Grubs survived Taster, they could fly up to the top and track them down. That was out of their hands, though, so Hondo oriented himself, and they started back along the edge to meet up with Horace and Byron.

Along the way, he kept edging closer to the drop-off. He didn't see any sign of Taster and Big Tom, but he didn't see any Grubs go spherical and float on up to get them, either.

They stumbled back upon a worried-looking Byron and Horace.

"Glad to see you guys made it, but what the fuck happened?"

"Did they record?" Hondo asked, ignoring the question and nodding to the instruments.

"Yeah, all sorts of shit. I don't know if it's any good, but we uplinked everything. What about the weapons? Did they work? Did the shitpods detach?"

"No. *Fucking* no. And they were on our asses all the way until Taster took them under fire with the ninety-six."

"Yeah, we heard that. I've been trying to raise him. And what the fuck happened to your face?"

"A Grub was what happened, what do you think? And I had to stim."

"Ah, shit. Did you put in a block?"

"Hell. No, I didn't."

It wouldn't do that much good, but he could stop the slow injection of stimjuice into his body. He'd feel a huge letdown, but he'd recover all that much faster.

Sitting down, Ben looked beat. He was going to collapse soon. Neither one of them were in shape to travel back to the podsuits at the moment.

"We're going to stay here for awhile to let Taster and Big Tom find us. Ben needs the rest, and I'm going to collapse. Good by you?"

Byron nodded and said, "Get some sucrose into you, then conk out. We'll keep watch until Taster and Big Ben get back."

Hondo took a tube of "sucrose," the sickeningly sweet calorie and supplement gunk that would help him recover, and then turned off the stim.

"Ask Taster to let me sleep for five hours," he said as his eyes began to feel heavy.

Ten hours later, the four teammates shouldered the instruments for the march back to their podsuits.

Taster and Big Tom had not shown up, and there was no sign of them. With heavy hearts, the four started the journey back to the Itch.

GOLDEN HAPPINESS STATION

Chapter 18
Sky

Sky leaned back in her chair and rubbed her eyes. A wicked headache was kicking in. She could zap it into oblivion with a shot of napostern, but she'd taken three already over the last six hours, and the doctor had told her to limit herself to two doses per day. Better to just grunt through it.

"So, Doke, run that by me again," she told Learned Jameson.

"The data all points to the fact that the S-Po did react as the one in our lab. It's connector pods relaxed in the same manner."

Sky didn't bother to correct Jameson. Almost everyone had started to refer to the D-Cells as S-Pos, and it didn't make much of a difference now. What she needed now were answers.

"So, if the S-Pos did react in the same way, then why didn't they detach?" she asked, for the fifth time in an hour.

"As I said, Vice-Minister, we haven't been able to determine the degree of reaction in the field test on the planet. It is possible that we didn't calculate the maximum distance to deploy the prototype. And we cannot forget that the operator did not follow the instructions that he needed to keep the S-Po under fire for a full twenty seconds," Willis Jain said.

"Oh, come on, Doctor. Do you really think three more seconds would have made a difference?" Olaf Kristenov snarled from across the conference table. "Didn't you read the regression numbers?"

"I'm not saying that at all," Jain said, looking like he was going rise to his feet. "But without experimental standards, we cannot conclusively formulate what happened. Or didn't they teach you that at Cambridge?"

"Gentlemen, stop!" Sky shouted as she rose. "We don't have time for your pissing contests. We need to get to the bottom of this now."

She stood there, hands on the table, her eyes on fire. Her head was splitting, and she didn't need to be listening to the two men square off.

"And as for you, Doctor Jain, that *operator* was a Federation Marine, and his *subject* was a twelve-meter-long nightmare Grub trying to kill him. I think we can forgive him if he missed three fucking seconds."

Twenty-three pairs of eyes swiveled to her as one, mouths agape.

Oh, don't give me that. None of you have ever cursed?

Ever since the accident, the morale of the team was crap. Harry O'Shaw had been well-liked and respected. Willis Jain had been especially close to Harry, and he'd taken the loss particularly hard. They all were depressed, both because of their losses and because of the fact that the prototype had failed. Rumor was that they were all about to be recalled and replaced, and that didn't help things, either.

If Sky was going to be replaced, well, that might be best for everyone, but until the hammer fell, she had to push, prod, and cajole the team to work together. These were some of the finest minds in human space, and they had to come up with a solution. If not them, then who?

"I want to hear something new, people. Let's look at this from another direction."

Her eyes drifted to Malcolm Orrisy. The young man, who'd been so brash and self-confident before, was more subdued now. His ego had taken a few hits, and he now realized that he was not God's gift to xenobiology. Still, he was brilliant, and Sky needed to harvest what he could offer.

"Malcolm, you've been quiet these last few hours. What do you think?"

"Ma'am?"

"What do you think? What do you think went wrong?"

"I . . ." he started before glancing hurriedly at the others, then lowering his head.

Are the rest still riding him? Sky wondered.

"'I' what, Malcolm?"

He looked around at the others, indecision on his face. Then a wave of determination replaced it.

"I think we're looking at this incorrectly. We're examining the data streams, but focusing on the S-Po. We need to look at the Dictymorphs, instead."

"We did. We got back the readings," Jain objected.

"Emissions, magnetronics, wave propagations, and everything else emanating from them."

"And?" Jain continued.

"And? Was that the only thing taking place? Jesus!"

He reached down and picked up a stylus, holding in in his open palm, then turned to Julia Hyperama and said, "Take this."

Julia recoiled slightly, then looked around the table in confusion.

"I said, take this, Doctor Hyperama," he repeated.

Julia looked at Sky, who nodded and said, "Take it."

With a shrug, she reached out to take the stylus. As soon as her hand touched it, Malcolm snapped his own hand shut, holding it tight.

"I can't if you do . . ." she started until it sunk in.

It didn't matter if the S-Po released its connection. Not if the Dictymorph wouldn't release it. Sky was shocked. It was too simple a theory, but it could be true.

"We all know that the connection is via the dovetail joints. If a Dictymorph can change its shape, then certainly it might be able to adjust the joints to keep the S-Po attached."

It made sense. Sky didn't know if that made it true, but at least it was something they could examine.

"So, how can we defeat that?" she asked him.

"I . . . I don't know," he admitted. "I'm a xenophysiologist, not a mechanical engineer. Joints and the like would be something for an engineer."

"Well, who here is a mechanical engineer?" Sky asked, looking around the room.

No one said a thing.

Hell, we're all theorists, she realized. *I need to send for one immediately.*

"Where can we get one?" Jameson asked.

"I'll . . ."

Where's my mind? I know where to get one. I know where to get a dozen engineers.

"We're on a space station. Who keeps this thing operating, people? Engineers, that's who. System engineers, electrical engineers, nuclear engineers, mechanical engineers. Hell, even the technicians who keep the machinery running.

"Malcolm, get together with Learned Jameson and Doctor Jain. I want a list of every kind of engineer you think you need and get it to me in thirty minutes. I'll get you your engineers, and I want a weapon out of you that works."

PROPHESY

Chapter 19
Hondo

Hondo stopped as he stepped out of the terminal. In the middle of the square was the 30-meter tall statue of General Ryck Lysander, Prophesy's most famous son. As a Marine, Hondo had a special place in his heart for the general and chairman of the Federation, the leader of the Evolution. The general's statues were everywhere, including the 200-meter colossus on Lysander, the planet named for him. Here on Prophesy, though, the general's homeworld, the impact was greater.

"You coming?" Lauren asked, turning around to see why he'd fallen behind.

"Oh, yeah. Sure."

They made their way across the square and through the crowd to the hyperrail station. He felt more than a little out of place. For the last two years, he'd been on the Itch, at *Golden Happiness*, or on Grub-held planets. Sure, *Golden Happiness* had a significant population, but it was a space station, and he hadn't seen crowds in a single place there. This was the first time he'd been under open sky with more than 50 or 60 people for a long while.

The only signs of the war were the recruitment posters on the government building along the north side of the square. People were going about their daily routine as if the universe was at peace. It was jarring to his sense of reality.

"I told you, Hondo. My dad's not that bad. He's not going to eat you alive, so don't be nervous."

Lauren had mistaken the cause of his silence. True, he was a little nervous about meeting Lauren's family, especially her father.

Commander Stephen Riordan, Federation Navy (Ret) had been a Shrike picket-skiff pilot, flying alone into the Black. Now, a successful businessman back on Prophesy, he was a man who had never known failure and didn't tolerate those whom he felt unworthy.

This was Hondo's first leave since joining first Marine Recon, then transferring to Interrecon. He'd contacted Lauren to see if she could swing leave at the same time only to be told that she was going to attend her brother's wedding and asked if he could come with her. Hondo had originally envisioned one of the leisure planets for a little fun, a little romance. Being a plus-one at a family gathering did not strike him as anything he'd want to do, but he knew that he was stuck. If there was a future to be had with Lauren, then he couldn't very well refuse. So, with a smile he didn't feel, he'd said of course, he'd love to come.

He tried to sound interested as Lauren excitedly pointed out her favorite pizza joint, her favorite sushi place, and her favorite starball cafe, the last being inside the station. She stopped, ordered two Hawaiian Sunbursts from the takeout window, and looked at him eagerly as he pulled the starball off the stick with his mouth. The look of approval in his eyes wasn't fake. This was a good, good starball. A broad smile broke out on Lauren's face as if she'd make the snacks herself. He ordered two more for them to take on the train.

They found two empty seats, sliding in while the rest of the passengers crowded on. Their bodies were pressed together, and Lauren kept putting her hand on his arm every time she wanted to emphasize her point. Hondo was *extremely* aware of her as a woman, but he tried to push any more intimate thoughts aside. He doubted that they'd have much of an opportunity to steal away for some private time.

They stood up at the third stop, pushing through the standing passengers and barely making it off the train before the doors hissed to a close. Hondo spotted Cara waving at them.

"About time you made it," she said, giving each of them a hug. "Mom's been hyper about getting you fitted."

"Whatever fits you is going to fit me," Lauren said.

"Ha! With these guns?" Cara countered, flexing her arms and kissing each bicep. "In your dreams."

"Like that matters," Lauren said, before turning to Hondo and saying, "You're lucky. You just have to sit in the audience."

The Riordan house was only two blocks from the station, and Hondo trailed the twins as they eagerly got caught up in all the family and local gossip. The highlight was that Justin—whether that was family or friend, Hondo didn't catch—had gotten two girls pregnant and proposed to both of them, all while he had a boytoy stashed in a downtown condo. Hondo thought himself above gossip and didn't want to listen, but he couldn't help it. This was *so* outside his worldview.

They reached the house, and Hondo met Commander Riordan before Lauren was whisked away to get her final fitting. The commander handed him a Corona—Lauren or Cara had obviously briefed him on what Hondo drank—and invited him into a mancave, where he took a seat on an overstuffed chair. He felt the arm of the chair. It might be actual leather, not that Hondo could tell the difference between leather and the high-end synthetics.

Hondo looked around the room. It was pretty righteous, he had to admit. There were 2D and 3D images on the walls, covering Commander Riordan's career as a Navy pilot. Plaques from a dozen units filled one entire section. Three intricate models of the one-man Shrike picket-skiffs were on the side tables. They looked pretty much the same to Hondo, but Cara had long ago told him that her father had flown three different models, including the DR variant—"DR" for "Deep Reconnaissance."

"Well, it is good to finally meet you, Staff Sergeant. I've heard quite a bit about you over the years, and not just from the girls. You've made quite a name for yourself."

"Sir? I'm just a grunt, nothing more."

"Just a grunt? Hardly. You don't need to show false modesty here. Be proud of who you are."

"No, really, sir."

"You earned a Navy Cross. That's not 'just a grunt.' And now, you're . . ."

Hondo wasn't sure if the commander was pumping him for information or not, so he said, "Sir, I can't discuss my current—"

"Relax, Staff Sergeant. I'm not prying. Hell, half of my career is still classified. I'm just saying that you've done well, but there's one more point, if I might add."

"Uh . . . certainly, sir," Hondo said, quickly taking another sip of his beer just to break eye contact with the man.

This is getting awkward.

"Cara thinks highly of you, and that would be good enough for me. But Lauren, she's not going to pick an also-ran. She'd only pick the best."

What? What's he talking about? We're just friends.

"I . . . I don't . . . I'm not sure what to say, sir," he stumbled out.

"Well, I guess the best does not necessarily mean you can speak coherently," the commander said with a booming laugh. "Cara said you can be a little shy, but I'd like to know you better, son. Why don't you tell me about Destiny? Cara's told me about the battle your two fought, but I'd like to hear your side. That's not classified, is it?"

"Uh, no, sir. I can tell you."

"Well, with the girls doing their thing, we've got time."

Hesitantly at first, but warming up as he got going, Hondo told his view of the fight. That morphed into a mission the commander had on Victorious 4, then on one of his deep space missions when his Shrike malfunctioned. Lauren and Cara's oldest brother Mark came in to be introduced, then took a seat as the stories continued. Some were a little farfetched, and if Hondo exaggerated his a little, well, that was because he was sure the commander was as doing the same.

There's a saying about the difference between a fairy tale and a sea story. A fairy tale starts with "Once upon a time," while a sea story starts with "This ain't no shit!" More than a few of their stories that afternoon were of the "This ain't no shit" variety.

The commander had just finished a story about a liberty port on Vegas, and the two younger men were roaring with laughter when Lauren poked her head into the room.

"Well, I see you three are getting along. What's so funny?"

The three looked at each other for a moment before simultaneously breaking out into laughter again. Lauren might be in the Navy, so she'd heard raunchy sea stories before, but that was her father, and that particular story was better left unsaid.

"It was nothing," Hondo said as Mark tried to choke back the laughter.

"Right, nothing. That's why you're all acting like twelve-year-olds," she said, rolling her eyes. "Well, we're back, and I want you to meet my mom. So, if I can steal him for a moment?"

Hondo got up, and as he was about to follow Lauren out of the room, the commander said, "Remember, mushy peas!"

Hondo couldn't help it. *Mushy peas.* He burst out into another bout of laughter, and a blob of spit flew out of his mouth, making a perfect arch and landing on Lauren's collar just as she turned back to him. It glistened as she glowered at him.

"Are you about done? I don't want Mom to think you're crazy."

"No, it just . . . I mean, your dad . . . and mushy peas."

"I know my dad. Just remember, half of what he says is utter BS."

As it should be when telling sea stories.

"I never heard whatever mushy pea story he told you. You'll need to tell me that one later," she said, intertwining her arm in his. "He can sure tell some good ones."

I will if I can figure out a way to clean it up.

Hondo's eyes were transfixed on the glob of spit on her collar. He needed to figure out a way to wipe it off, but he couldn't with her grasping his arm.

"After you meet Mom, we've got two hours before the rehearsal dinner. The wedding's tomorrow. Then on Monday, Mark, Bev, and the kids are going up to the cabin, and they've asked us to go with them. They want to get to know you. Cara's going, too."

Hondo stopped dead, pulling Lauren to a stop, too. The cabin was a one-room dome on some mountain lake, he knew. A *one-room* cabin? For five adults, if they joined them, and four kids?

The two of them were leaving Prophesy on Friday, and Hondo did not want to spend his time on the planet is a very crowded one-room cabin, no matter how beautiful the view supposedly was.

"What?" Lauren asked. "You already like Mark, I can tell, and you'll love the kids. They'll be all over you."

Hondo stared at her, his mouth gaping like a goldfish's. His mind was blank.

"Oh, look at your face, Hondo," she said, pulling him in for a quick kiss. "You'd have thought I just sentenced you to 20 years in prison.

"Yes, Bev did invite us, and we could go. But there are rental units on the other side of the lake. Very quiet, very private units. With big Jacuzzis in each one. We can go up there, or we can stay here in the city. Your choice."

"Private? As in just you and me?"

"Yes. Just you and me."

Hondo pulled her in tight, his arm squeezing her waist and said, "That was pretty mean, CT2 Riordan. I think it was against the Harbin Accords, treating me like that."

"Oh, so you are a prisoner of war?" she asked, squeezing him back just as hard.

"Only a prisoner of your heart," he said.

Oh, my freaking God! That was so lame. Why the hell did I say that?

Hondo and Lauren had been easing their way into a relationship, but Hondo was not the most demonstrative guy in the world. He'd never been much on compliments or flowery speech, and here he finally said something, and it sounded like it came out of a telenovela.

If Lauren thought it was lame, however, she didn't show any sign of it.

She pulled his head down and whispered into his ear, "And I'm going to keep you prisoner, so get used to it."

Hondo felt his heart pound. It was out in the open now. He turned her around, and they came together in a long, firm kiss.

She broke first, wiped her mouth, and said, "Later, big boy. Now, let's go meet my mom. She's more than a little anxious to see who's stolen her daughter's heart."

GOLDEN HAPPINESS STATION

Chapter 20
Skylar

The Dictymorph simulacrum quivered at the blast. Immediately, the Bosch & Wipro tech checked the readouts, both on the Dictymorph and the new S-Po simulacrum. The tech had been forced upon the team by the admin types after the previous damage to the original simulacrum. Sky waited impatiently for her OK, and finally gave the team the go-ahead.

Malcolm, Olaf, and Jerri St.Giles, one of the station's mechanical engineers that had been assigned to the team now, were running this test, which coupled the previous detachment beam with a shock wave. The idea was to make the S-Po release, and at the same time, physically jerk the S-Po's connectors out of the Dictymorph's receiving slots. The S-Po hadn't detached from the larger Dictymorph. Sky hadn't expected it to—they were using relatively weak charges—but that would have been a welcomed development.

The Green Team huddled around their data readouts, heads together as they discussed the results. Sky couldn't tell from their posture or gestures if the results were promising or not.

"What do you have?" she asked, running out of patience.

Olaf looked up as if surprised at the audience filling the room.

"It looks like we have achieved some detachment. Approximately eighteen percent. But most pairs are still connected."

"And is that a matter of the strength of the shock wave?"

"Yes and no. I mean, probably, but there is more to it than that. The detachments were all centered around the alpha point."

Which made sense. The alpha point was the aiming spot, so to speak, of the beam. This was the point of aim for the beam and the paired shock wave. The number of successful detachments, though, was disappointing.

"It doesn't matter. This is never going to work," a voice said behind her.

She turned to see who spoke. It was one of the engineers, Frank or Francis Something-or-other. Sky had seen the man around, but she'd never talked to him. He kind of looked like a bum, unkempt and sloppy, and Sky had avoided him.

"We just have to increase the power and widen the focus," Olaf objected to what the man had said.

"Why won't it work?" Sky asked Frank/Francis.

"Oh, the theory is OK. And we can rig something up that will overpower those simulacrums. But those won't be practical. You have to remember that these need to be incorporated into weapons that our soldiers can use. That, or we need monster projectors, and we've seen what the Grubs can do to those. 'Sides, no matter how you skin this cat, the range is going to be limited. Dissipation, you know."

"Right now, we're working to validate the theory," Olaf said, looking a little indignant. "Once we do that, we can work on a practical weapon."

"You can't beat physics. Limits are limits. You've already validated the theory, at least on a big doll. But keeping on with your means of deployment, well, that's just a waste of time."

"And just why won't we be able to make this work?" Olaf challenged.

"Jus' look at the numbers, man. Orrisy there, he calculated that it'll take two thousand kilopascals to break the Grub's grip on the shitpod."

Sky winced at the term "shitpod," but Malcolm nodded.

"At best—at say, 100 meters in an Earth-like atmosphere—a man-packed system using today's technology might be able to generate a tenth of that, and only at the alpha point."

Sky pulled up the man on her PA. Frank Pullman, a master hydraulic engineer.

Hydraulics? What do they know about this type of physics?

She turned to Sister Keiko, who had grown into her second-in-command, and quietly said, "I want someone to refute or confirm what he's saying."

Then she asked the man himself, "So, Mr. Pullman, are you saying this is a dead end? That we should stop this line of research?"

As if that is going to happen just on his say-so.

"Not at all, Vice-Minister. We just use a different method of employment."

"Like what?"

"We already have it. Two-hundred-and-ten-millimeter shells. We use them to throw meson beams downrange. We can get that projector down to size without too much effort, then throw in a concussion charge. Boom, the round hits, and we've got a hundred-meter radius that will knock the hell out of the shitpods."

"I thought you said that a hundred meters wasn't very good," Malcolm said.

"It's shit for a point target, especially when you're the soldier that has to fire the weapon. But this is a sphere with a hundred-meter radius. Everything in it is hit, and you don't have to worry about alpha points."

"And you said we have these shells already?" Sky asked.

"The shells, yeah, we do. Not the guts. Take out the meson generator, replace that with the new innards, and we've got tens of thousands of them. Maybe more."

All eyes turned to look at her. Sky had to think. She had more Ph.D.'s with her than she could shake a stick at, the best minds of humanity, and here was an engineer, telling her they were going about it all wrong? Although nothing he'd said jumped out at her as being incorrect.

"Anybody got an objection to what Mr. Pullman has said? Any obvious flaws?"

No one said a word.

That didn't make the man right, but she could not ignore the possibility.

"Mr. Pullman, which team are you on now?"

"Blue."

"OK, starting immediately, I want you on . . . on Gray Team," she said, choosing a color that had not been used. "I'm going to shift some people to Gray, and you are going to help them figure out a way that we can get this weapon into a shell."

She'd get together with Sister Keiko and decide who to send to Gray. Some might think an engineer was beneath them, but Sky didn't care. She'd assign anyone as she deemed fit if it would get the results.

"Green, I want you to continue on your present course, no change, but I want you to provide any assistance the Gray Team needs.

"Let's buckle down on this, people. And let's think things through before we move forward. We probably jumped the gun on the last field test, so check and recheck. We can't take forever, but we've got time to do it right."

EARTH

Chapter 21
Skylar

"You have no more time," the secretary-general told her. "The situation is coming to a head, and we need a solution."

"Yes, sir. I understand. We just don't know if our current direction is feasible."

"Look, Skylar. If this is beyond you, tell me, and I'll put someone in your place who can manage it. We all respect what you've done for the war effort. I respect you. But your understanding of the Klethos and bringing the Brotherhood back into the fold did not take the same skills that managing a research lab requires. You are here to be my advisor. I've given you leeway to remain on the station, but I'm not seeing anything for all of that."

"We've made a lot of progress, Secretary-General," Sky protested.

"And so has everyone else. We've got twenty-eight labs working around the clock, but in case you haven't noticed, that clock has just struck midnight. We need an answer."

The secretary-general's midnight comment might be hyperbole, but if it was, it wasn't by much. The Dictymorphs had initiated a much more intense, broader offensive. Hundreds of thousands of them had hit twelve planets simultaneously: five Klethos and seven humans. The entire human and Klethos military were being mobilized to meet the threat, focusing on the more populated worlds, but the initial battles had resulted in defeats. All the new weaponry was being neutralized by the extra energy supplied by the S-Pos.

"What about Boston Arms?" Sky asked. "Have they made progress?"

Boston Arms was an extremely secretive corporation in the Confederation. They'd been working on weapons designed to exploit what some of the other labs were discovering, but they were not sharing much of their own research.

"Constant improvements of existing weaponry, but nothing on the S-Pos. That is the key right now. So, once again, I ask you, do you have a solution?"

"The chances were good. With another test—"

"For God's sake, Skylar. Haven't you been listening to me? We don't have time for another test. Upwards of sixty-million people have already been killed, with millions more each day. We need it *now*."

This wasn't the way R&D was done. This wasn't how weapons systems were designed. There were procedures in place, and they were there for a reason. The field tests on D39 and D504 had shown that there were usually failures before there were successes. That was why they called them "tests."

But the secretary-general was right. People—and Klethos—were being killed. They had to act, and act now.

"We're ready," she said with conviction. "We have 200 shells ready to test, but Zhou Junbei can ramp that up immediately."

She hoped they could, that was. Zhou Junbei, LLC was a very high-tech armament company, but they were not known for their mass-production capability.

"My question to you is, will they work?"

She barely paused before she said, "Yes, they will. I'd stake my career on it."

The secretary-general frowned and said, "Your career is the least of my worries. You are staking millions of lives on it. We have limited resources, so I need to decide where to use them."

Sky felt more than a little ashamed of her "career" statement. The secretary-general, who looked like he'd aged a century over the last few years, was worrying about the trillion humans whose very lives were at risk.

Am I putting personal pride over everything else?

She gave it a moment's thought. Jorge McAllister, Taterville's director, was sitting in the outer office right now waiting to see the secretary-general. Before she went in, Jorge had confided that Taterville's sonic-based research was leading nowhere. At MIT, Irina Delray-Bolton was months away from a possible solution. The remaining 25 labs that the secretary-general mentioned were focused on more conventional methods to fight the threat, from combat weapons to biological procedures.

Ego aside, the research on *Golden Happiness* was the closest to being able to handle the S-Po issue. The military needed an answer if they were going to be able to push back the Dictymorphs. If Sky and the *Golden Happiness* team couldn't give that to them, then quarantine was the only answer.

Sky shuddered at the thought. "Quarantine" was a nice euphemism for planetary destruction. Humans had done it once, and many factions that were safe back here on Earth were proposing to make that a matter of course. They wanted to vaporize any planet the Dictymorphs attacked, killing every living creature on it— thereby make the Dictymorph body count too high for them to want to continue their wave of conquest.

The problem with that was two-fold. When Purgamentium had been vaporized, that had probably taken the Dictymorphs by surprise. They had proven to be remarkably reactive to human action, changing their tactics as necessary. Having once lost thousands of them on a planet, Sky was certain that they would be taking precautions.

Second, "every living creature" included humans. Over eight billion people lived on the seven human planets that were now being attacked. Eight billion. Destroying those planets would kill hundreds of thousands of Dictymorphs—at the cost of those eight billion souls.

The chairman had briefed her personally on this, calling it the Hellfire Option. Told to keep it a secret, she was the only person in her teams, as far as he knew, who knew the consequence of losing the fights for the invaded worlds.

"Well?" the secretary-general prompted her.

There was really no choice. Eight billion loves lost was simply too large a number to even comprehend. The shells they'd been developing were their best bet.

"Yes, we're ready."

God help us if I'm wrong.

OSIRIS

Chapter 22
Hondo

The predawn sky lit up as the thousands of pieces of flaming debris arched down to the planet's surface, spread out over a hundred square kilometers. In amongst the debris were what was left of more than 6,000 Marines. Hondo fell to his knees, gut-punched.

Ninety-thousand Marines were already on the planet, and more were in orbit, ready to land. It looked like the Grubs had other ideas, though. For the first time, they had opposed a landing. They had shot down one of the big Navy troop carriers, which had been in low orbit while shuttling the Marines to the surface.

Six thousand Marines and another 400 sailors, gone, just like that.

Hondo leaned over and threw up, his body wracked with spasms, until nothing more came up, and he thought he was going to rupture his throat. Four hands reached over to hold him until the spasms stopped.

"I'm OK, Ben. Thanks," he said before washing the bile and acid from his mouth with a swig of water.

Hondo had seen death. He'd lost friends. Here on Osiris, he knew that millions of civilians had been killed already, but this had hit him on a visceral level. He didn't want to know which units had just been wiped out. There was no doubt that he knew Marines who'd been aboard the cursed ship, and right now, he had to clear his head and get back in the game.

In the distance, smoke started to rise from fires started by the remains of the ship; a stark reminder that once again, the rules had changed. This time, though, he hoped the Marines would be making their own changes. Hondo and Ben were there to help make it happen.

That is, if the battery was OK. They'd been in the general area of the debris field.

"Copper-three-three, are you OK?" Hondo asked over the fire control net.

"That's affirmative Crow-four. It was a near-miss, but we are operational. The mission is still a go."

"Roger. We are still a go," he replied, then turned to Ben and said, "They're OK."

"Then we'd better be ready," Ben said as if he was simply telling Hondo that is was time for lunch.

Hondo's mouth still tasted vile, and his gut was sore from the wrenching. He wished he could compartmentalize all the bad things that happened like his friend could. It would make life easier.

Surrounding the two teammates were the 12,000 Marines of Task Force Juarez. Their job was to close with the approximately 4,000 Grubs that had been ravaging the AO. Two cities with a combined 70,000 souls had been leveled and destroyed by the time the Marines landed, but as cold as it might sound, that was a sunk cost. Those lives were lost. Now, the Marines had to somehow maneuver the Grubs into a position where not only could the arty rain down their new shells on the Grubs, but the infantry could then close in and destroy them before they had a chance to recover.

That was easier said than done. The Grubs weren't cooperating, moving haphazardly, and engaging Marines as they could. The arty battery was constantly on the move, trying to be in position for when the call came. And Hondo and Ben were the eyes and ears of the battery, ready to call for fire or get them out of the way of a Grub advance. Those 34 Marines were vital to the success of the mission in this AO, and they had to be kept out of the Grubs' reach.

"Did any Grubs get squashed by the debris?" Hondo asked Ben.

Acting as forward observers for arty was not their only mission. Once again, Interrecon was lugging scientific instrumentation, ready to uplink the data of what happened during the artillery barrage. That equipment was helping them monitor the Grubs' positions.

Ben lifted his upper arms at the elbows in the Klethos version of a shrug. It would have been too much to hope for, Hondo knew.

"So, let me take a look at where they are," he said, getting up and moving to the instrument suite.

There were a half-dozen concentrations of Grubs in the AO, the largest looking to number about 1,000. Second Battalion, Seventeenth Marines was playing cat-and-mouse with them, trying to lure them into the artillery ambush while Third Battalion lurked out of reach, ready to pounce after the barrage. All the time, the battery kept moving, adjusting its firing point. It was a chess match, but one that was taking its toll.

One Grub had been killed by a massive mine, and others had some of their energy stores depleted, but 104 Marines had been lost. At some point, they had to engage decisively for real, or they would continue to be picked off one at a time.

It had to be difficult, Hondo knew, for 2/17 to keep playing the rabbit. The entire ethos of the Marines was to close with and destroy the enemy, not to play pattycake with them and lose fellow Marines in the process.

Ben tapped the ground display. A smaller group of about 90 Grubs had changed direction, and they could become a threat to the battery. Ben pulled up the drone feeds, but as expected, the folder was empty. There had been 958 drones of all types launched over the AO. Currently, eight were still aloft but shut down by the squadron. There were no overt signs that the Grubs had shot them down, but that was the logical conclusion. Once they began to fall out of the air, the squadron had tried to take the others offline in order to save them for when they could contribute the most to the battle. They hadn't saved many. With the Navy ships pulling back now, that left ground sensors such as Ben and his suite the eyes and ears of the task force.

"Copper-three-three, we've got approximately ninety Grubs at twenty-one klicks to your two-nine-zero. They are currently on a one-four-zero heading, I repeat, one-four-zero heading."

"Roger that, Crow-four. I have ninety at our two-nine-zero, heading one-four-zero. Wait one."

If the Grubs kept moving in that direction—which was hardly a done deal— they would pass within 14 kilometers of the battery. That would be beyond the range at which the Grubs typically fired upon ground troops, but as every ops plan briefer stressed, they could shoot down Navy ships in orbit, so they had the potential to engage ground troops at much longer ranges than they had been doing.

"Crow-four, we are displacing to five-four-eight-eight, nine-seven-three-two," Copper-3-3 passed as the new position appeared on Hondo's ground display.

The new position would not only take the battery farther from the 90 Grubs, but would put them in a better position to initiate the ambush on the larger body. Hondo zoomed out his display to take in the bigger picture. The cat-and-mouse game he was observing looked to be the closest to come to fruition, but that was only in their AO. Across the planet, there were more battle areas. He didn't know what was happening in them. He didn't know if other batteries had fired, and if they did, whether the new wonder shells had worked or not. He was painfully aware that the lives of 20 or 30 million civilians and 90,000 Marines probably depended on the shells.

If they didn't work, then the Marines would have to engage the powered-up Grubs. Hondo thought they could still prevail, at least in their AO, but it wouldn't be easy, and Task Force Juarez would be decimated. If Task Force Cancun, some 2600 clicks to the planetary west, started to fall to the 8,000 Grubs in their AO, then the TF Juarez survivors wouldn't be in much shape to reinforce them.

"Let's displace, too," Hondo told Ben. "I want to be closer, so we can help out if needed."

A good thing about their current suite was that it had fewer instruments than they had humped before. It had all been mounted on a commercial frame that still had the Outdoor Living stock tag on it. The entire suite came in at 104 kg—light enough for Hondo to hump, but barely a burden to Ben. The instruments didn't even have to be shut down. With Ben on point, Hondo could bring up the rear and still have eyes on the display.

It would be better yet if he could cast the suite displays to his PA, but no one had acted on the suggestion he'd made in every after-action report he'd submitted. It wasn't as if it would be a difficult mod. There were more than enough casters in the commercial world, and they could be modified for military use easily enough.

Hondo and Ben moved quickly, almost at a jog, through the yew scrub. Osiris was primarily a mining planet, but it has been completely terraformed. The 1.12 Earth gravity was a little heavy for some of the big conifer forests so loved by humankind, but there were vast tracks of smaller-bole trees. Hondo had initially assumed that redwood and fir forests would be better places to fight the Grubs, but that had proven not to be the case. Grubs could maneuver easier in the spaces between the forest giants. In yew, white pine, and larch forests, the trees were too strong to simply be bowled over by a Grub, but too densely packed for them to wend their way between the trees. The advantage was that the two warriors could move without fear of running into a Grub.

While they humped, he monitored the battery's position vis-a-vis the 90 Grubs, but the closing distance never got below 17 klicks. Two hours later, the two reached his selected position just as an element of 2/17 opened fire on the Grubs again. They two stood silently as light tendrils and explosions reflected off the bottom of low-hanging clouds, like a far-off lightning storm.

They were too far away to see or hear the fight, but Hondo knew that men—and hopefully Grubs—were dying under those clouds. Bit by bit, 2/17 was getting worn down. This couldn't go on forever.

Ben dropped the instrument panel, and Hondo studied the ground display, which provided much more detail than his monocle. The main body of Grubs was centered 52 klicks from his and Ben's position. Two-Seventeen was 43 klicks away, and heading towards the battery, with 3/17 bird-dogging their sister battalion 20 klicks to their east. To the west was a vast track of the same dense forest that he and Ben had been pushing through.

"This might be it," Hondo said as he studied the display.

"Why do you think that?" Ben asked, stepping up beside him.

"Look. The Grubs are following two-seventeen. If they keep following for another five klicks, they'll be in range of Charlie Battery. Over here," he said, "the trees are just like the shit we went through, too dense for the Grubs unless they ball-up and fly over. And if they do that, then they've got no cover for the Tridents."

The Trident was a new weapon, put out by Boston Arms, specifically designed to attack Grubs when they were in their spherical form and flying. They'd proven to be effective, and each battalion had two launchers with 120 of the weapons each. Between the two battalions, that meant 480 "spears." That wouldn't be enough enough to take out the entire force even if they somehow managed a one-trident, one-kill ratio. They'd devastate the Grubs, however, and the Task Force commander would jump on that chance.

"Now, they've got Three-Seventeen here to the east, ready to take them on. So, they have to stay here," he said, pointing at the area running from 15 to 30 klicks in front of Charlie Battery.

"If that were a Klethos company, we'd just push the attack, either to Three-Seventeen or straight ahead. Take it directly to the enemy."

Ben's "we" was a stretch, as no male Klethos were in the fighting companies, but what he'd just said was essentially what was the standard Marine immediate action drill if caught in an ambush: assault through the kill zone.

"True, but all we need to do is to get the Grubs inside an artillery kill zone. We need to hit them with these new shells, then we *want* to close in with them. All those PICS Marines down there, they are loaded for bear," he said, patting his M96. "They've got the M191 in their Weapons Pack Threes now."

The M191 used the same technology as his M96, but instead of a 46mm, 785g round, the M191 fired a massive 118mm, 6.8kg round. The rounds were still in limited quantities, and the PICS Marines so armed had been held back waiting for the artillery ambush, but Hondo was sure the weapon would prove deadly.

"I'm loaded for bear, too," Ben said, patting his M96, modified for a Klethos grip.

Hondo laughed. Ben had been confused by the term the first time he'd heard it, but now his teammate seemed to enjoy the phrase. He sometimes referred to the Grubs as bears now.

Hondo kept a wary eye on the 90 Grubs who seemed to be moving erratically, but not getting closer to the battery. His attention was centered, however, on the larger body. Every minute, they moved closer to the ambush. He could feel his pulse rising along with the stress level. So much was riding on whether the new artillery rounds worked or not.

He checked the status on each of the instruments one more time. All were green. Hondo wasn't sure how they would be able to tell if the shitpods detached or not, not from 30 klicks away and not even line-of-sight. The techs had told him not to worry about it, but he did. If 3/17 rushed in like the cavalry, but the Grubs still had the shitpods, then things were going to get ugly very quickly.

The worst part of all this was that Hondo and Ben had no input into the situation. Sure, they had to make sure the instruments didn't turn off, but as far as the coming battle, they were not going to be part of it. There was nothing that either one of them could do to affect the outcome.

"It's all falling together," Hondo said, trying to will the Grubs closer.

The ground display showed greater detail, but it didn't show casualties. Hondo flipped down his monocle and pulled up the numbers. One-hundred-and-nineteen Marines had now fallen—and as he watched, one more was KIA. The CO was playing a knife's edge game. She had to keep in enough contact with the Grubs to keep them coming, but she couldn't risk total engagement yet. It was a fucked-up position to be in.

"Come on, anytime now."

Hondo didn't have all the command and control features, but the Grubs were all within range of Charlie Battery's twelve tubes. He wasn't sure why they weren't firing yet.

He glanced back at the suite's ground display for a moment. The 90 Grubs were splitting up . . . no, they were circling something. But what?

The ground display was filtered for Grubs and human military. Osiris had large herds of deer and other Earth animals roaming the wilder areas, and having it register all life, even large life, could make it confusing. Wondering what the Grubs were doing, he started to remove the filters.

He didn't have to go past the first one. The Grubs were surrounding hundreds of civilians who were taking refuge in a dense marsh. He repositioned the cursor on the instrument that measured Grub energy emissions over the center mass of the humans, and the numbers jumped. The Grubs were firing at them.

"Ben—" he started, before being cut off.

"Crow-four, we are about to commence fire. We need you start sending your fire missions."

Hondo looked back at the display where civilians were being slaughtered. His entire purpose in life was to protect civilians. It wasn't just lip service—it was how he defined himself, as a protector of the people. But he had a mission right now, one he had to fulfill.

With a huge effort, he wrenched himself away from the civilians and passed, "Roger that. We're ready."

He turned up the gain on the ground display, and thirty seconds later, the report of eight volleys of twelve rounds each reached the two—a *bump, bump, bump* that he could feel in his chest as well as hear. Ten klicks away, the rounds arched up and out, targeting the mass of Grubs.

"We're ready. Get that to us as soon as you can."

If the Marine on the other side of the connection sounded anxious, that was to be expected. Hondo had seen what the Grubs could do to artillery pieces, and it wasn't pretty. The battery would fire two more salvos based on Hondo's input, then displace.

Hondo counted the seconds. The rounds should land 26 seconds after firing. At 21 seconds, light tendrils reached up in the distance. The Grubs knew there was incoming. They question was whether they could do anything about it. The rounds were not guided. There were no emissions. They were simply letting Osiris' 1.12 Earth gravity take them to the target.

Five seconds later, the first salvo started to impact. On the ground display, small red rings, each representing a circle 240 meters in diameter, bloomed on the display. Grubs within any ring were switched to a dull yellow. Those outside of any of the rings were kept a bright red. The battery fired so quickly that Hondo couldn't keep up. More and more rings blossomed, more and more Grub avatars switched to yellow. Not all of them, though. After the last volley landed, 48 Grubs were still shown in red.

Hondo's fingers flew, tapping each red spot. That was forwarded to the battery, and their targeting AI started working out firing solutions. Two more volleys reached out.

"Thanks, Crow-four. We're displacing."

"Did it work?" Ben asked. "Are the shitpods detaching?"

"I don't know. I don't know how to read these figures, but 2/17 has stopped and turned, and here comes 3/17. We're going to find out soon enough."

GOLDEN HAPPINESS STATION

Chapter 23
Skylar

"Did it work?" Sky asked. "Are the S-Pos detaching?"

Two batteries—one Federation Marine and one Alliance of Free States Army—had fired within the last minute, the first two batteries to do so. Sky had asked that all shells be fired simultaneously to better block a possible Dictymorph defensive reaction, but she'd been roundly ignored by the UAM military. Captain Lamont, her Federation military liaison, had told her to expect that—it was pretty much an impossible request given the realities of combat.

"We're running the data now," Julia said.

Sky wrung her hands. The waiting over the last two days had been almost too much to bear, but the last two hours had been even worse. The chairman had called her twice, and the secretary-general three times.

And now, she'd know. Over 200 shells had been fired. So much depended on what happened on two worlds so far away.

Weighing on her was the knowledge that the chairman had shared with her. If they could not stop the Dictymorphs on the seven human worlds that had been invaded, then the Hellfire Option would be employed. This was no longer simply a possible course of action; the decision had been confirmed that the Dictymorphs would be stopped, one way or the other. And if "the other" meant destroying the worlds, then that was a price which had to be paid.

As far as she knew, no one else in the room was aware of what would happen. It was all weighing heavily on her shoulders. This simply *had* to work.

"It looks . . . it looks like we have detachment!" Julia said as the room erupted into cheers.

"Really? How many? What's the rate?"

"There are some fuzzy numbers, but on Procolyn 3, it could be as high as ninety-two-point-six percent. And here are the numbers from Osiris coming in: ninety-five-point-four percent!"

A wave or relief swept over her. It worked! Her PA was buzzing with calls from the secretary-general and three heads of state.

She knew the battles on the twelve worlds, human and Klethos, weren't over. They hadn't even gotten artillery on the sparsely populated K58 and Robert's World. Even where they had the artillery shells, all they'd done was help even the playing field. The real fighting was still going to rely on the individual Marines and soldiers. That was where the war was being fought.

All around her, people were cheering and hugging each other. She'd let them have their moment, but then it was back to work. They needed to provide the fighting men and women not only the means to level the playing field, but to tilt it in the humans' and Klethos' favor.

OSIRIS

Chapter 24
Hondo

Hondo watched as 2/17 stopped and turned, taking a fixing position while 3/17 moved into the assault. Operations never worked out as planned, but from the readouts, this looked as if an animator had laid out the entire thing. It was beautiful. The question was what would the Marines see when they closed with the enemy: Grubs with or without their shitpods?

With their prime mission finished, Hondo and Ben were now free agents: a resource for the task force commanding general. They would do whatever they could to help advance the overall mission.

Hondo zoomed out on his display to try and get an overall view of the AO to see where they might be needed, and his eyes drifted to the trapped civilians, and—"

"Copper-three-three, I've got a fire mission for you," he passed as his fingers flew, designating targets.

"Uh, Crown-four, we're displacing, and not by echelon. We are not that effective while on the move."

"Well, you better damned well get effective, 'cause you've got ninety Grubs heading your way."

"What? What do you mean?"

"I mean, you've got ninety Grubs making a beeline for you right now. That concentration I told you about? They're heading your way."

"Are you sure?" the Marine on the net asked, her voice cracking.

"I'm sure as shit. I think they've got a bead on you."

"Uh . . . Crow-four, wait one, over."

As he studied the readout, he realized that what he'd said wasn't quite true. Four Grubs looked to be staying in place with the civilians. Eighty-five were heading towards the battery. The Grubs advanced past the targets he had highlighted, so he cleared the screen, switched to tracking mode, and then hit them all again. With the last one in the call for fire queue, he hesitated only a second before tapping on the four Grubs that had stayed back. They might not pose a threat to the battery, but they were a huge threat to the civilians.

"Crow-four, we are halting four tubes and beginning a displacement by bounding overwatch. Request you act as forward observer."

He hit the send, then said, "You should have the target list now. Please confirm."

"Roger, we have them. First rounds downrange in seventy seconds."

If they can get the first rounds out in seventy seconds, then they're hot shit.

The battery was self-propelled, but only as a matter of moving the tubes. They were not designed to fire while on the move. It was possible, but accuracy suffered.

Hondo had given them the targets along with a time-track so that they could determine the speed of the Grub advance. With that, they could fire their guns so the rounds hit where the Grubs would be at splash.

In theory.

A change in speed, a change in direction, would throw that off. The drones they had sent aloft to do the targeting had been knocked out of the air, so they were blind. And that was why he and Ben had to act as forward observers, letting the battery know what was happening.

On his monocle, Hondo watched as six tubes stopped and got ready to fire while the other six continued. They would displace another 500 to 1,000 meters, then stop and fire while the first six-gun platoon displaced back past them to set up another two-to-three klicks beyond. This would allow one platoon to fire at all times.

Right at seventy seconds, Hondo heard the soft reports of outgoing rounds in the distance. He started a timer, watching the big ground display that showed the Grubs on it. He'd forgotten to ask for a time-of-flight, and he wasn't going to call up now. At 30 seconds, he started to get antsy. At 40, he was downright nervous. At 47 seconds, explosions sounded as the first salvo hit.

Red rings blossomed on the grand display. Two rounds landed north of the mass of Grubs, with another four along the northern edge, and Hondo sent the correction. The firing at this point was AI-controlled, so he didn't have to speak over the net. Fifty seconds later, six rounds landed right in the middle of the advancing Grubs.

He hit the fire for effect command. This would have to be approved by the battery commander, so he keyed back on the mic, and then said, "Good shooting. You're right on target."

"That's a no go on the F-F-E," the Marine passed. "We've got forty-eight rounds left. We have to go sniper now."

Which Hondo knew meant "one-shot, one-kill." And which was not how the queen of battle fought. Artillery covered wide swathes of ground, sweeping it with hot shrapnel. If he and Ben had to essentially aim those arty rounds, then the situation was pretty dire.

Ben tapped a clawed finger on the four Grubs that had remained behind.

Shit, we've got to do something about that.

He quickly designated them, then passed, "We need rounds on G-Eight through Eleven."

"That's a negative. Those four are not a threat at the moment. We will continue with the rest."

"Copper-three-three, be advised that those four have over a hundred civilians trapped and are systematically killing them. Those people need some help."

"Roger, understood. Wait one."

Hondo understood the situation. If the battery fired four rounds at those Grubs, then that would leave them with 44 with which to defend themselves. If they were overrun by the Grubs, then that could have a long-term effect on whether the planet itself could be saved.

He waited as the seconds dragged on, and finally, he heard a "Rounds downrange" a few seconds before he heard the reports themselves.

"That's all we can spare, Crow-four."

"Roger that, and I appreciate it."

Ten seconds later, they fired another four rounds, this time at the main group of Grubs, which had started to pick up speed. Hondo watched the display, half-holding his breath, until the rounds splashed—each of the four hitting right on the targeted Grub, the red ring on the display encompassing each one.

"Fucking-A yeah!" Hondo shouted.

If the rounds worked as advertised, then none of those four would have their shitpod. They could still kill civilians, but this gave the people a better chance, even as shitty as that was.

And then the rounds landed among the main body of the Grubs. More of the Grubs were within the ECR of the rounds, and Hondo quickly adjusted the targets to hit the ones that probably still had their shitpods.

"Look at that one," Ben said, pointing.

One of the Grub avatars on the screen had stopped while the rest continued on towards the battery.

"Copper-three-three, I think you ghosted one of them. It sure isn't moving," Hondo passed excitedly.

"Really? Great, only eighty-four left, then. And we've got thirty-two rounds left, so, I bet we can get them all," the Marine said with more than a trace of bitterness.

Shit, I didn't think that one through before saying it like that. They're in a pretty tough spot, and here I am, gloating.

He didn't know what to say, so he stayed off the net, adjusting the calls for fire to those Grubs that had not been within a round's ECR. He sent up the targets, then waited for the splash. More Grubs were within the ECRs, but not as many as there had been before when they were more bunched up. He kept highlighting those that had not been hit, then left it to the arty firing AI to determine how best to allocate the remaining rounds.

"Copper-one-one's out of rounds," Copper-three-three passed after the next volley. "We're displacing now. Copper-one-two will be up in five mikes, so wait for their confirmation. Copper-three-three, out."

Hondo wanted to ask Copper-three-three her name, but it was too late. She'd cut the connection. She'd been his contact in the battery, probably a sergeant within the battery FSC. He was surprised to hear that she'd stayed with the first gun section instead of with the company headquarters.

The lead Grubs were less than six klicks away. The platoon was just within the normal operating range of the light tendrils. If the Grubs spotted them, then there wasn't much the section could do to defend itself. The gun chassis were lightly armored against small arms, but that was about it.

And they still hadn't started moving. Hondo was not a gun bunny, but he'd watched artillery displace before. The spades—which gave the piece stability against the recoil—had to be recovered, and the tube needed to be stowed for travel, but it shouldn't take that long. At last, one of the pieces started to move, but then it stopped again.

"Get the hell out of there," Hondo said.

And then it hit him. He was afraid to look, but he had to see. The third display identified Grub energy expenditures. The numbers were all over the chart, but with 3/17 and 2/17 engaging, that was to be expected. Hondo drew a circle around the 84 with his finger, then dragged it to the search box. The numbers were still spiking.

The Grubs already had the first platoon under fire.

"Mother fuck, those bastards!" he said as he jumped up and paced back-and-forth.

"That is a warrior's purpose," Ben said, standing to the side.

"Shut the fuck up, Ben. That was not their 'purpose.' They'd already done that with the main body. This shit," he said, pointing at the instrument suite, "served no fucking purpose. And what do I do? I get them to waste four rounds on Grubs that weren't chasing their asses to kill them."

Ben said nothing but simply watched Hondo pace.

Hondo knew that last was bullshit, that he was just venting. They had to protect the civilians, and if the first gun section was gone, then it hadn't been for "no purpose." They had at least delayed what was happening to the civilians, and they'd managed to detach about fifty of the shitpods—if the damned rounds even worked.

"Crow-four, this is Copper-three-six. What's the status of the Grub advance?"

"Copper-six" would be the battery commander.

"The status is that they just took out your first gun platoon. I don't think any of them made it."

"I know. Where are the Grubs? I only have the last positions you sent to Copper-three-three."

"You know?" Hondo asked, wondering how the man could be so calm when he'd just lost half of his battery.

Shit, of course, he knows, and he's just trying to deal with the situation.

Unlike Hondo, the battery commander would be linked to each of his Marines, so he would know immediately when one of them was killed or wounded. He knew his platoon was lost, and had known from the second it happened.

"I need the positions, Marine," the commander said.

Hondo slapped his face hard, then shook his head.

"Roger that. Sending now," he passed.

"Received."

"Sorry I yelled at you," Hondo told Ben as they waited for the next message.

Ben tilted his head in the Klethos shrug.

"No, really. It was unprofessional."

He almost wished that Ben would just yell at him or make some snide remark. He felt it hanging over them. But Ben was as placid as ever.

"Crow-four, we are going to hit them with an FFE with two salvos when they reach First Platoon. I'm going to need an immediate BDO and positions so we can fire our final two. Understand?"

"Roger that. But, your position, it's . . ."

"It's within their range, yes, if we wait that long, but that will give us the best opportunity to hurt them before Golf 2/17 can get here."

Hondo quickly zoomed back out. There was movement of a Marine unit, not towards the main body of the Grubs, but back to these 84 Grubs. He made some quick calculations, but it was obvious that the 2/17 PICS Marines could not make it back before the rest of the battery was engaged.

"Understand, sir. We're here for you."

"Just be our eyes, Crow-four. Help us take out some of the bastards."

"Roger that." He started to key off, but then he asked, "If I can ask you, what was Copper-three-three's name?"

There was a pause, and for a moment, Hondo didn't think the captain was going to answer, but he said, "Arabelle. Sergeant Arabelle Tiburon."

"Thank you, sir," Hondo said, before turning to Ben and asking, "Did you hear that?"

Ben shook his head. The Klethos had learned that humans shook their heads to say no, and they'd readily taken to it.

"They're going to fire on the Grubs when they reach the dead Marines."

"Why not now?"

"Because they only have twenty-four rounds left, and the commander hopes that the Grubs will bunch up at the platoon's position."

Which could be true. Grubs tended to keep firing into their targets, even when a target was no longer in the fight, so they might zero in on the tubes, even if they were already out of action. That wasn't always the case, but it was as good as a plan as any.

"We need to get the BDO to him as soon as possible, so they can fire off a second salvo."

Hondo wasn't really going to send up an actual Battle Damage Assessment. He wouldn't know, for example, whether the shitpods were even detaching. But he was going to send up what targets still had to be hit, and the intent should be the same.

Hondo continued pacing, stopping every minute or so to check the progress of the Grubs. They were moving quickly, closing the distance to the battery's First Platoon. Twice, the battery commander called to check the progress as well. Finally, the Grubs looked to be about a minute out, and Hondo called it in. Twenty seconds later, he heard the muffled reports of two salvos going downrange. He watched the ground display, trying to will the rounds on target.

It was a righteous effort, perfectly spaced to maximize the coverage without overlap. Many of the Grubs already "hit" were within the ECR of these rounds, too, but 28 more were successfully targeted. That left 12 that were still untouched: 12 that still had their shitpods. Hondo's fingers flew as he highlighted the 12, then sent that on up. Ten short seconds later, he heard the final two salvos fire.

The battery was out of rounds. Hondo didn't know what weapons they had for self-defense, but he knew it wouldn't be enough. Their only hope was to get the hell out of there and hope that Golf Company got there in time.

Before the rounds landed, the battery was on the move, heading to meet Golf. It took the Grubs only a few seconds, and they started to adjust their heading.

"Shit, that's going to screw up the targeting," Hondo said.

But then the final 12 shells started landing. Five more of the untouched Grubs fell within the shells' ECRs. If the new weapon worked, that meant most of the Grubs had been stripped of their shitpods. That didn't mean they were harmless. Hondo had fought "normal" Grubs before, and they were deadly. As if to emphasize the point, one of the mobile artillery pieces stopped moving, almost assuredly taken out by the pursing Grubs.

He wished there was something he and Ben could do, but they were too far away. Even if they could get there, he wasn't sure they could do much. Their M96s were effective weapons, and they had incendiary grenades, but that wouldn't do much against 84 of the enemy.

But what about four of them?

He zoomed in on the trapped civilians. There were far fewer of them showing up on the display, but some of them were still alive. Someone had been smart enough to get everyone to disperse within the densely packed trees, and the Grubs looked to be roaming the perimeter, firing into them.

He checked the distance. If they ran—and abandoned the instrument suite—then he thought that they could get there in 30 minutes. That might be too late to save anyone, and even if they got there in time, a human and a Klethos against four Grubs were not good odds, but he had to try. They couldn't stand by and do nothing.

"Do you want to go fight some Grubs?" Hondo asked Ben, pointing at the display.

Ben had been calm for the last hour, almost withdrawn, but at Hondo's question, he perked up, his neck frill rising.

"*Irassis*," he blurted out.

Hondo didn't know what "*irassis*" meant, but by looking at his partner, he was going to assume that was a "yes."

"Then let's go kick some Grub ass."

Chapter 25
Hondo

The Grub fired another tendril into the brush. Hondo still had his monocle, but without the instrument panel, he couldn't see the civilians, so he didn't know if someone had just been killed or not. He didn't know if there was still anyone alive at all, but he had to go with the belief that there were still survivors, people who needed Ben and him.

The best piece of news was that the Grub didn't have a shitpod attached. If it had one in the beginning, then the artillery had stripped it of the organic powerpack.

He was still breathing heavily from the run. Ben, laying next to him, didn't look winded at all. His neck frill was twitching; the only sign that he was excited.

When they had taken off, the four Grubs had surrounded the civilians, who were scattered in a rough oval, 450 meters by 200. They only had the one in front of them, 220 meters away. Hondo couldn't see the other three, but he could see it when they fired into the trees.

He wasn't sure why the Grubs didn't simply crash through the trees and root out the civilians. They could knock down a wall of a building with their bulk, but three-meter-high trees kept them out? Sure, there were a lot of the trees, which looked almost too dense for humans to take refuge in them, and a hundred twigs were stronger than a single branch, but still . . .

He wasn't going to question good luck, though. If they stayed outside of the yew forest, then it was all the better, both for the people and for Ben and him to target them.

"OK, let's start with two rounds each. That should be enough to put it down. On my order," he told Ben.

With a target as big as a Grub and only 220 meters away, Hondo could hit it with his eyes closed. Still, he took careful aim, sighting on the thing's center of mass.

"Ready?"

"Ready," Ben replied.

"On three. One . . . two . . . three!"

Hondo fired once, reacquired the target, and fired again, all within three seconds. Ben took two. All four rounds arched slightly over the ground and slammed into the Grub, which contracted immediately into a sphere and let out a piercing squall that hurt Hondo's ears, almost vibrating his brain inside his skull.

The Grub re-elongated again, and without turning around, charged Hondo and Ben, light tendrils dancing towards them. One hit him, momentarily blinding him as his cerrostrand armor managed to deflect it. To his right, Ben fired twice more, and as the rounds hit, the Grub slopped forward another 20 meters, deflating. The body spread out, limp and lifeless.

"Thanks, buddy," Hondo said, breathing hard.

He hadn't trusted the shielding woven into his utilities, but it had saved his life. He still didn't want to stand up to a direct hit, but it did offer some protection.

"Let's go!" he said, getting to his feet and running forward with Ben on his ass.

A light tendril reached over the trees from the other side, but missed them by ten meters. Once again, he was grateful that, as accurate as the light tendrils were against planes, spaceships, and even tanks, they were not as deadly accurate against personnel for reasons which baffled him. He guessed that it was like using arty against ground troops as a direct fire weapon—not accurate, but deadly if it hit.

He was supposed to be the team leader, but he really didn't have much of a plan. Not that he had many options. They could try to keep on the outside, circling around to engage the Grubs, but if the shot that had been fired at them from over the trees was any indication, then they wouldn't be able to surprise the others. The other option was to get inside the trees and use them for cover.

It seemed to take them forever to cover the 250 meters to the treeline, and Hondo kept expecting more light tendrils to come seek them out. Halfway to the relative safety of the trees, Hondo hit a muddy patch and slipped, landing hard on his ass and knocking the breath out of him. Ben swept him up, almost carrying him for a few meters until Hondo could get his feet beneath him.

Hondo hit the tree line, bursting through the first line before getting wedged between two close trees. He had to jerk himself several times to break free.

"No wonder the Grubs didn't follow," he muttered. "It's tight as shit in here."

A few meters to his left, Ben was struggling. His wider frame and four arms were hanging him up, and he was swinging his arms almost as if he were swimming to burrow further in.

"Slow down, Ben. Go easier," Hondo said as the tree trunk beside him blasted apart in a shower of splinters.

The same shielding that diverted a Grub light tendril did nothing for the wood that smacked Hondo in the face. He recoiled as blood started to flow. Another round whizzed by him, and he dropped to the ground.

"Cease fire, cease fire!" he yelled.

There was another shot, and he heard Ben grunt in pain.

"I said cease fucking firing! Are your fucking deaf?"

"Who are you?" a wavering voice called out.

"We're not fucking Grubs, that's for sure!"

He heard the sound of muffled voices, then, "Who won this year's pickball championship?"

Hondo rolled his eyes and fought to keep control of himself. There was a very frightened person there; someone he'd come to protect.

"I don't even know what pickball is. I'm Staff Sergeant Hondo McKeever, United Federation Marine Corps. I'm here to help."

"And what is that thing with you?"

Oh, come on, everyone in human space can recognize a Klethos if they ever see one.

"That's Ben. He's a Klethos, and he's on our side."

There were more muffled voices, then, "Stand up and let me see you."

"OK, I'm standing. But don't fire."

Just my frigging luck. Survive the Grubs, but get ghosted by a settler.

He slowly stood up.

"Come forward," the voice said.

Hondo waved at Ben to stay down, then took five steps forward through the trees. There, using a tree trunk as cover, was a young girl, probably no more than ten or eleven years old. She held an ancient-looking slug thrower on him, the barrel steady and unwavering. On the other side of the tree, in full view, were two younger boys, one wringing his hands in nervous fear.

A man's body lay on the ground behind them, unmoving.

There was a flash of light, a tree exploded nearby, and the boys cried out in fear. The girl kept the rifle aimed right at him.

"Can you put that down, miss?" he asked, keeping his voice calm and gentle.

She looked at the two boys, then slowly lowered the weapon.

"Can you help us?" she asked, sounding very, very young.

"Yes, that's why we're here. I'm going to tell Ben to come join us, so don't be afraid, OK?"

"OK, sir."

"Ben, come on over."

The girl started to raise the rifle again as Ben stood pushed his way forward. Hondo interspaced himself between them. Ben's upper right hand was mangled, but he didn't show any sign of pain or even anger.

"Remember what I told you. Ben is here to help you, too."

"Are you really a *d'relle*?" the older of the two boys asked, using the term for a Klethos warrior who used to fight humans in the ring.

"I am Klethos, but not a *d'relle*."

"Did you fight Duchess Ruby?" he asked.

Duchess Ruby was a fictional gladiator, the hero of a very successful Hollybolly franchise. Out here in the Far Reaches, flicks like that might be how people formulated their understanding of the Klethos.

"No, I did not, young man."

"Good," he said.

All three children had almost obsidian-dark skin, and the dead man looked more Asian, but Hondo asked, "Is that your father?"

"No," the girl said. "That's Mr. Tony. He was taking care of us when he got kilt. So, I had to take his gun."

"And you did a good job. What's your name?" Hondo asked.

"Tammy."

Another tree exploded, but a little farther away. The Grubs were still attacking, and Ben and he needed to take the fight to them.

"OK, Tammy. I want you to stay here. Don't move until someone comes and gets you, OK?"

"You're leaving?" she asked, panic setting in.

"We have to. We'll be back, though. I need you to be brave, OK?"

"OK," she said, sounding unsure of herself.

"Does that hurt?" the older boy asked, pointing at Ben's hand, which was dripping blue blood.

Hondo hadn't even asked Ben about it. The hand was mangled, just bits of tissue barely held together.

"Yes, it does," Ben said matter-of-factly.

That was probably an understatement. The Klethos upper hands were the sensitive hands, full of nerve endings to allow for fine manipulation. It had to hurt like a son-of-a-bitch. He seemed to be handling it, however, so the two of them had to push on.

"Let's go," he told Ben.

The older boy rushed out and grabbed Ben's leg as the two started to move out. Klethos did not tend to touch each other as a rule, and they avoided physical contact with humans. Hondo didn't think that Ben would do anything, even if the boy's sister had just shot off his hand, but he instinctively took a step back to Ben as his teammate knelt beside the boy.

"What is your name, young man?"

"Winston," the boy said.

"And your brother?"

"He's Richmond."

"Well, Winston, I need you to stay back here and take care of Richmond. Do what your sister tells you, and we'll talk later. Can you do that?"

Winston seemed unsure, but he said, "Yes," as Ben gently removed the boy's hands from his leg.

Hondo felt guilty for his reaction. He trusted Ben with his life, but at a gut level, there must be something going on there. He'd immediately moved to protect the human boy from his Klethos partner.

"Let's move," he said to Ben, trying to clear that thought from his mind.

The two had just started off when a crashing through the brush stopped them. It wasn't a Grub, so it had to be human. Two men appeared, weapons raised.

"Who shot . . ." they started before seeing Hondo, in his very obvious military kit, and Ben standing behind him.

They stopped, mouths open, before the lead man said, "Who are you?"

"Staff Sergeant Hondo McKeever, United Federation Marine Corps, and this is Ben, my partner. We're here to help. We've taken out one Grub already," he said, tilting a head behind him.

"You took out the one to the south? Like kilt it?"

"Yeah. KIA."

The two men exchanged looks, and then the first one said, "We're really glad to see you. How many of you are there?"

"Just us two."

The man's enthusiasm faded, but the second man said, "They kilt one, Leo, and that's more than we've done."

"That's true enough," Leo said. "Can I ask you to come with me? Tabitha's going to want to parley with you."

Before Hondo could answer, Leo saw Tammy and asked, "Tammy girl, where's Tony?"

"Kilt," she said, pointing to the body, the line-of-sight from him to the dead man blocked my Hondo.

Leo stepped to the side and saw the body.

"Ah, hell," he muttered, then, "Elijah, can you stay with the Parker kids while I take them to Tabitha?"

"Sure thing."

"Are you coming?" Leo asked Hondo, studiously ignoring Ben.

Hondo nodded, and the two teammates followed the man deeper into the trees.

"How many of you are still alive?" Hondo asked as two more light tendrils struck nearby, exploding trees.

"Don't 'zactly know. Tabitha, she tolt us all to scatter when the Grubs hit us. Still, we were goners for sure until the explosions, and most of the devils left."

"That was a Marine Corps battery," Hondo told him.

"Whoever it was, I want to buy them all some beers, if we ever get out of this mess."

Hondo didn't tell him that the Marines in the battery were all likely dead.

The three passed four bodies lying in a jumble on the ground. An overweight woman was on her back, slightly apart from the others, her pink blouse burnt, silent hands reaching for the sky. Most of her hair was gone, and the smell hit Hondo hard, almost making him gag. The other three, possibly a man and two other women, were bloody messes. The two shattered trees told the story. If the tendril hadn't killed them, then the shards of wood had finished the job.

"Tabitha, I'm coming in with a Federation Marine and a . . . and his partner," Leo called out.

Most of the stand of trees consisted of yew, but Leo pushed through a stand of some shrubs that Hondo didn't recognize. Hondo followed, entering a small clearing. An ancient woman, her hair ice-white, stood up to greet them. She was barely 1.6 meters tall, and possibly 35 kgs soaking wet.

"I'm Tabitha," she said, her hand out to take his, her incredibly blue eyes making Hondo wonder if they were color-modified.

When Ben pushed through the shrubs, she barely hesitated, dropping Hondo's hand and shaking Ben's as well.

"What's your unit . . . uh . . . son?" she said, her eyes searching for his rank insignia, something they didn't wear in Interrecon.

She knows something about the military, he realized.

"I'm Staff Sergeant Hondo McKeever, United Federation Marine Corps," he said for the third time in ten minutes. "This is Ben, my teammate. I'm afraid it's just us."

Her intensely blue eyes dimmed slightly when he said that.

"They kilt one of the Grubs, Tabitha."

"Is that true?" she asked. "You kilt one?"

"Yes, ma'am. The one to the south of us here."

She considered that for a moment, then shook her head and said to herself, "Not enough."

"Not enough what, ma'am?" Hondo asked.

"I can see you're some sort of special forces, so you must have been around. Have you fought the Grubs before?"

"Yes, ma'am. Many times."

"So, tell me, are these gonna stick around and keep chipping away at us?"

Another explosion, this one quite close, served as an exclamation point to her question.

"Probably. They can tend to get focused on whatever's in front of them."

"But we had a hundred of them chase us in here. Then almost all of them left," she said.

"Because they had a bigger target—the Marine battery. They left four back here because, quite frankly, that's all they figured it'd take."

"So, we can't wait them out. We've already lost so many of us. I hopt if we disperst, they wouldn't waste their time. We're not a threat to them."

"I don't think they differentiate between soldiers and civilians, ma'am."

"With the one they kilt, can we try for the cave?" Leo asked.

"I don't think so. The one to the west will mow us down like wheat. You saw what happent before," she said.

"Cave? What cave?" Hondo asked.

"We were taking Petersford Landing—that's our town—and trying to get into Latoya's Secret when the Grubs caught up to us. That's a cave," she added, when she saw the confusion on Hondo's face.

"The opening's like way wide," she said, holding her hands about a meter-and-a-half apart.

"How deep is it?" Hondo asked.

"No one knows. No one's ever made it to the end. Pretty blushing deep, though."

"How far from here?"

Tabitha looked at Leo, then shrugged and said, "Maybe two kilometers? A little less?"

"I didn't see any hills that close," Hondo said.

"It's not in no hills. It drops into the ground," Leo said.

Hondo pulled down his monocle and searched the map of the area. No caves were shown.

"Can you show me . . ." he started, before he realized how stupid that was.

It wasn't as if Leo could point it out on his monocle image. He knelt, then scratched out a rough oval on the ground. He put an X where the dead Grub was, then small O's where the other three were. A flurry of light tendrils dance into the trees for a few moments as he drew, but he ignored them.

"Can you show me on here where this cave is?"

Leo and Tabitha looked at each other, then Tabitha said, "I haven't been there for years. You show him."

Leo pulled down on his lower lip for a moment, his eyebrows scrunched together, then he reached out and put his finger on a spot. Given the size of the oval Hondo had drawn, that meant the cave would only be 500 meters away, which he already knew was wrong. He took the same rough azimuth, then took it out to represent about two klicks.

Tabitha was correct. If this were an accurate representation, then the Grub to the west would be able to take anyone running to the cave under fire. It would be a slaughter.

Staying in the trees would be slaughter, too.

"How many people do you have in here that are still alive?" he asked Tabitha as someone in the near distance started screaming in pain.

"Too few," she said bitterly. "We left PL with four-hundred-eight-four. I think over four hundred made it into the trees here. After that? Fewer than two hundred, I'd be guessing. That's all."

Hondo pulled up the task force intel net and subvocalized into the mic, saying, "Eagle-two-two, this is Crow-four. I've got two hundred, that is two-zero-zero civilians at this pos. They are under attack by three Grubs with over fifty percent casualties so far. Can you provide relief?"

"Wait one, Crow-four."

Hondo had expected that. The S-2 would not have the authority to dispatch a relief party—that would be the S-3 or the task force commander. Hondo zoomed back out to get an idea of the scope of the battle. He didn't have a very detailed view, but it looked like the two battalions in the AO were heavily engaged.

"Crow-four, there are no units available. The Three will try and break something out when he can, but I have no ETA yet. Suggest you take cover until then."

Hondo had expected that as well, but he'd had to ask. Looking at what was happening, he didn't think that cavalry could arrive sooner than two or three hours at best.

"How much longer do you think we can hide out in here?" he asked Tabitha.

There was another explosion, followed by cries.

Tabitha looked straight into Hondo's eyes, then said, "Twenty, thirty minutes. I don't know."

"Then, if you don't mind, this is what we're going to do."

Chapter 26
Hondo

"Just a little farther," Monica said as they low-crawled through the trees.

Hondo could see sunlight passing through the branches, so he knew they were close. Another tendril cracked overhead, passing to strike somewhere behind them.

"OK, wait here," Hondo said.

He checked his load. He had 16 rounds of the 46mm rounds left. He wished he had a hundred.

"You ready, buddy?" he asked Ben.

Ben slowly raised his neck frill to its full extent. Beside him, Monica let out a little gasp. It did look menacing, Hondo had to admit. Ben faced front again, and his frill settled back over his shoulders.

I'll take that as a yes.

His palms were sweating, and he tried to wipe them on his utility trou. The waiting was always the hardest part when excitement and battle lust warred with fear. Once the fighting started, the warrior in him would take over, he knew. But at the moment, fear was winning out.

A good part of that was fear for his safety, he acknowledged, but the bulk of that fear was if he'd made the right decision. He hoped he hadn't sentenced over 200 people to death. That was making him tremble as he waited for the signal.

It's a pretty fucked up plan, he had to admit.

They didn't even have comms. All commercial communications systems had been cut off, and the only military comms were what he and Ben had. He'd contemplated sending Ben with the main group so that they could communicate, but he needed Ben's 96.

He looked over at his partner again. He'd gotten his right upper hand bandaged, but the bandage was soaked in his dark blue blood. A Klethos could fire the weapon with either the upper or lower arms, but they were more accurate with the fine-motor upper arms. When Hondo had asked him, Ben had curtly assured him he was combat-ready and good to go.

Just when Hondo thought he couldn't take it anymore, a blast from an air horn reached over the stand of yew to them.

An air horn, for God's sake. That's what we've been reduced to.

"Let's do it," Hondo told Ben.

Together, they crawled forward the last five meters until they could see out of the trees and saw . . . nothing.

Shit, where is it? Has it moved? Is it going for the air horn?

Another tendril fired, coming from Hondo's right. He rose up to one knee, and 250 meters away was their target. As he watched, it fired another tendril. Hondo ducked back down, then motioned to Ben, who nodded.

No one completely understood how a Grub targeted people. They could move right past someone as the ones on G8 had done and never make a move, or they could reach out and take out a single human at seven klicks. These Grubs seemed to be firing at random into the trees. Hondo had a sneaking fear that they were simply holding the civilians in place until the others, the ones that had gone to take on the battery, returned. Holding in place or not, however, they were still killing the people of Petersford Landing.

Hondo mouthed "Ready?" and then silently counted down. When he reached "one," both teammates rose as one, sighted on the Grub, and then fired three rounds each. The Grub swung toward them just as Hondo fired the third round, and several pseudopods started to swivel toward them when the rounds hit. The Grub's body rippled twice, then exploded in a fury of light and pressure, the shock wave almost knocking Hondo off of his knee.

"Now, Monica."

Monica stood up and blew her own airhorn, three long blasts.

There was no turning back now.

"Move it!" Hondo shouted, and the three stepped into the open, outside the tree line, and started running south as fast as they could. Monica, who'd been picked for her speed, darted ahead. After the first rush of adrenaline, Hondo started to suck a little wind, but he kept up the pace. Ben took the rear, where he kept swiveling his head and body to see if the other two Grubs would pick up the chase.

Ahead of them, a line of bodies streamed out of the woods. Too few, Hondo thought. He was hoping to see more than 200, but the number was probably half that. A light tendril reached over the trees from the north but hit the ground 30 meters from the nearest person. That didn't stop the screams, though.

Monica reached the group and disappeared from view. It took Hondo another thirty seconds to reach the first of the people. He spotted Tabitha's white hair and ran up.

"Is this everybody?"

"I hope so, but I doubt it. Some might be hurt back in there."

Hondo and Ben waited as more people emerged from where Tabitha had staged them. It was taking too long. The two remaining Grubs could simply circumvent the trees and be among them.

"This was a bad idea," he muttered.

"Help me!" a middle-aged woman shouted at Hondo as she half-dragged, half-led a man out of the trees.

His left leg was useless, and he couldn't stand. Hondo automatically stepped forward, then pulled back. He couldn't get burdened by anybody. He and Ben were the only defense against the Grubs, and they had to cover everyone. If he was carrying another person, that could spell disaster if—no, *when*—they were hit.

"Sorry, I can't. You'll just have to make it happen."

The woman looked shocked, then said, "Piss on you, then, you Feddie piece of shit."

Hondo wanted to protest, but he couldn't take the time.

"Come on, come on. Move it!" he shouted into the trees.

Five armed civilians, including Leo, emerged.

Leo said, "I think that's the last of them."

It probably wasn't, Hondo knew, but the Grubs would probably abandon the woods now, so if anyone was left, they could be recovered after the Marines prevailed.

Not if, but when. We will defeat them, he told himself.

Nothing else was acceptable.

The mass of people was moving. Those in the front were running, those in the middle were more at a walk, and a good 20 or so were stumbling along. Pulling up the rear were the five armed civilians and the two Interrecon teammates.

Light tendrils started falling among them. Hondo didn't think they were aimed, yet three times, they hit amongst the people. A dozen fell, with only two getting back up and staggering on.

Hondo had expected to see the two Grubs within a few minutes, but the time stretched to five minutes, and then to seven, before Ben said, "Hondo, to the east."

Hondo stopped and spun around. One of the Grubs was rounding the trees.

"Keep going!" he shouted at Leo and the others as he and Ben took knees. Just a little farther forward and the Grub would be within range.

Leo and the others joined him and Ben, taking knees, and raising their old slug-throwers.

"You can't hurt them with those!" Hondo shouted. "Get the hell out of here!"

"But do they know that?" Leo asked, a smile on his face.

Hell, they're giving the Grub more targets so Ben and I will have more of a chance.

He didn't try to argue. The five had made their choice.

And paid for it.

The first tendril splashed the rough line, killing Leo and the woman next to him. The other three started firing. For any decent marksman, the Grub was too big to miss even at this range. Hondo couldn't tell if the small rounds even bothered the Grub, but its next tendril hit one of the others dead-on. The tendril then started to sweep towards the next person when Hondo said, "Now, Ben!"

Hondo fired four rounds.

The person whom the light tendril was tracking down broke his nerve and tried to dive out of the way. He screamed as he was hit just as Ben and his rounds struck the Grub.

It stopped, then shot a tendril that fizzled out within seconds. A stronger tendril reached out, splashing to Hondo's right.

"Die, you bastard!" Hondo shouted as he fired two more rounds.

He wanted to see it explode. He wanted it to be blasted into nothingness. He didn't get that. It deflated, disappearing from sight behind the contours of the ground between them.

Hondo stood up, glaring at where the Grub had been. He was tempted to close the distance—to make sure the thing was dead even if he had to empty his magazine into it.

"Hondo, there's one more. We've got to protect these people," Ben said, bringing him back to reality.

Leo and one other had been blown apart, but the third civilian looked like he might be resurrected. Hondo told the last man to carry him. Worlds like this rarely had full facilities—and if they did, they were usually not for the settlers—but Hondo wasn't just going to leave him.

It didn't look like his buddy were going to allow that either. He picked the man up in a fireman's carry and started jogging to catch up with the rest. Hondo and Ben brought up the rear, oriented toward the Grub that was somewhere behind them. Several times, light tendrils reached out for them, but without accuracy. The Grub was still there, and Hondo didn't know what it was planning, but for the moment, it was only taking pot-shots at them. As Hondo only had five more rounds, he was good with that.

It took 35 more minutes for the two partners to reach the cave. Leo had been right. It was barely a cleft in the ground. Hondo wasn't surprised that it had not been annotated on his map. He and Ben stopped just short of the cave, then provided security while people were helped into the cover of the ground. If it went as deep as Tabitha had said, then they should be safe from anything other than a full-on Grub assault.

The third Grub never attacked, and over the next few hours, the sound of fighting reached them when the wind was right. There were flashes in the distance, but he didn't know if those were from Grub or human weapons.

Just before dusk, eight shapes appeared on the horizon. Hondo stood up, and with Ben at his side, went out to meet them.

"Are you McKeever?" one of the Marines asked over his PICS external speakers.

"Yeah. And who are you?"

"Faisel Del Rio, from Golf Two-Seventeen. We heard you had a Grub problem, so here we are."

"Golf? Did you get to Charlie Battery in time?"

It was difficult to see any kind of bodily expression when someone was in a PICS, but Hondo could imagine that he slumped a little before he said, "Not for everyone. Those gun bunnies sure put up a good fight, though.

"But what about you? Where are the civilians?"

"Down there," Hondo said pointing. "We had four Grubs. Took out three, and the other, I don't have a clue."

"The two of you, you took out three by yourselves?"

Hondo could hear the disbelief in the Marine's voice. He wasn't surprised. PICS Marines tended to think that anyone not in a PICS wouldn't be able to accomplish much, especially against a Grub. Hell, Hondo was as surprised as anyone that they were still alive.

"Yeah. We had a little help," he said, thinking about Leo and the other two, "but yeah."

"Ooh-rah, McKeever. I heard about you, of course, but that's still righteous. And I wouldn't worry about that last Grub."

"Why not? Did you get it?"

"Didn't have to. They left."

"What do you mean, they left?" Hondo asked.

"Just that. We were kicking ass, and then, about two hours ago, bam, they all rose up and left. It was a turkey shoot. We blasted them out of the air. Some got away, but not many."

"What, did they consolidate or something? In our AO or one of the others?"

"You don't get me. They left the frigging planet. First in our AO, then, from what I heard, from every AO."

"What about the other planets? Where they invaded?"

"Hey, I'm just a staff sergeant like you. Cary Khat, by the way. I don't know about nowhere else, just here. And here, they're gone."

"Gone?"

"Yeah, we won, Marine. We won."

EARTH

Chapter 27
Skylar

Sky didn't even have time to check into the hotel. As soon as the shuttle landed, she was whisked to the Federation wing of the UAM complex. She was scanned three times as her escorts waited patiently, which she thought was excessive, given that the escorts weren't scanned at all. Could anyone think she was a spy who had somehow subverted them into escorting her in?

She was in a good mood, however, so she put up with it. She'd been in a good mood for quite some time now. When the Dictymorphs started evacuating Procolyn 3, she had been hopeful. At least one world had been spared the Hellfire Option. A few hours later, they started had evacuating Osiris.

On both planets, the human forces had been gaining the upper hand, thanks to the new artillery shells. But then the Dictymorphs had evacuated Little Bend, where the fight was still in question. Within hours, all seven human planets were devoid of Dictymorphs—even Robert's World, which had been quickly lost to the enemy within the first day.

To Sky's welcomed surprise, the Dictymorphs had even left the five Klethos worlds they'd invaded. She didn't understand why they had left, but she was sure happy with the outcome. Once all of this was confirmed, she had collapsed in her bunk for 13 hours of uninterrupted sleep before coming back to the lab to oversee the vast amount of analysis that was being done. They had to understand just what had happened. The Dictymorphs had suffered a couple of losses on a planetary level, but that didn't mean they had been defeated. Humanity had to understand why they left so they could react the next time they came. And they *would* come—of that, she was sure.

The recall had come at an inopportune time, but she'd half-expected it. There was going to be a conference on what to do now, and both the chairman and the secretary-general wanted her there. Still, she was feeling so good that she didn't even mind.

She was escorted to the chairman's office and was sent right in to see him.

"Skylar, welcome back," Chairman Hrbek said, coming around his desk to shake her hand.

"Thank you, Mr. Chairman. I'd like to say I'm happy to be back—"

"But you don't want to lie to me," he finished for her with a laugh. "Don't I know it. But I'm glad to see you. The conference is going to be, well, interesting, I would have to say."

"Like the old Chinese curse, 'May you live in interesting times.'"

"Yes, you understand my meaning, Skylar. Which is why I wanted to talk to you before it opens in . . ." he said, looking at his PA, ". . . in forty-three minutes. You like cutting it close."

"I'm sure there are others who still haven't arrived yet for the convocation and opening statements."

"True, but I want you there for the entire thing. I'll be there, of course, for the public parts, but you know as well as I do that the real work will get done in the breakouts."

"Sir, before we begin, can I ask you, to what degree have the Dictymorphs withdrawn?"

"Well, that's a good question, one that . . ." he said, before shaking his head. "Hell, you're as cleared for this as much as I am. Sorry.

"According to our Klethos friends, they've pulled out of sixty-three worlds, all which were outliers in Klethos space."

He flipped on his room suppressor, then raised a map of the galaxy over his desk. "These in red were the Dictymorph-held worlds before they pulled back."

Most of the red swatch was towards Andromeda, but quite a few—Sky would hazard a guess that the number was 63—were interspaced within the green of Klethos worlds. The chairman ordered the projector to show the current positions, and those 63 planets changed to green, showing a unified spherical wall of red worlds adjoining the Klethos part of the galaxy.

"They're building a border," Sky said.

"Exactly, and if you notice, we've got the Grub-held area in red, the Klethos-held in green, and little old us, here in the blue."

Sky bit back her natural correction on the "Grub" comment. Terms had meaning, and she didn't like the sloppiness of slang, but she could see what the map showed. The Dictymorphs were on one side of the galaxy. The humans were on the other. In between, was a thin line of green: the Klethos.

If the Dictymorphs were going to come back to attack humanity, then they had to go through Klethos space to get to them.

"And what is the Klethos position right now?" she asked.

"I see you understand the issue. Our liaison quad is making noises that they will be leaving soon. Some of our experts think the Klethos consider the war over."

"I don't buy that. We don't know how many Klethos worlds the Dictymorphs still hold."

"Worlds they took from other species."

"That doesn't matter, Mr. Chairman. They consider them Klethos worlds, and it will be a matter of honor to them. They have to take them back."

"Do you think they will attack right away?"

"No, I don't. They may be honor-bound, but they're not stupid. They're going to want to make sure they can win before they try to recover their lost worlds."

"Then why does it sound like they're pulling back from the alliance?"

Sky hadn't been prepared for that question, so she had to think for a moment before saying, "We still know next-to-nothing about their government. One thing we do know, however, is that honor is paramount to them. Would it be possible that—just as with humans and the Brotherhood—there are factions that don't want to cooperate with the humans? At the risk of anthropomorphizing them, what if some resent the fact that they had to come to us, an inferior species, to help save them from the Dictymorphs?"

"OK, so what if they have a faction that resents us?"

He was simply throwing the question back at her, but that was just his style, something she'd learned over the last several years.

"Once, again, this is pure, off-the-cuff conjecture, but if the Dictymorphs have pulled back, then this faction—if it even exists— might want to distance themselves from us. They might feel they don't have their life-and-death imperative to accept help from anyone else now."

"Do you think that's the case? I mean, do you think the Grubs have quit their war of conquest?"

"No."

"Well, you didn't hesitate even a second on that answer. Why do you think that?"

"We didn't defeat them, not in the classical sense. We had two planets, Procolyn 3 and Osiris, where it looked like things were going well for us. But nothing was clear on the others. Heck, we'd already lost Robert's World.

"Now, look at all that red," she said, pointing at the map still hovering above his desk. "And that is all we know. Do you think with all of that, they are going to let the loss of two worlds change whatever drives them?"

"Maybe they think they've run up against someone stronger than them."

"Maybe, but I'm betting that they are retrenching. They've demonstrated the capability to adjust. I think the latest assault was only a probe, to feel us out, to see what they could do. When they got that answer on Procolyn 3 and Osiris, they had what they needed. Now, they'll try to figure out a counter."

"And the sixty-three planets?"

"It makes sense from a military standpoint. The military calls that a salient," she said.

"Not quite a salient, in the classical sense of the word, but I get your point, Skylar. And you've brought up a few interesting possibilities. It just so happens, that they buttress, rather than refute, what I was going to bring up next."

Sky waited, wondering what the chairman was going to say.

"Our alliance with the Klethos has basically been in mutual support, but still separate. We have a few exceptions, but that is the way we've worked this. So, my question to you is, in your opinion, is whether we can integrate our forces."

Integrate? We tried that, and it didn't work out that well. Still, the Interrecon—with the less-aggressive and honor-bound males—seemed to have worked.

His question revealed his real plan. If they could integrate forces, then the Klethos would be wedded to humanity. Those green planets would be a buffer between the Dictymorphs and human space. If they could organize better and develop the Navy so that it could oppose the Dictymorphs, then future battles might be able to be limited to Klethos space. Human worlds would not have the threat of the Hellfire Option hanging over their heads.

"With the warriors, possibly. We tried that before, and it was not very efficient. It would take some time, I think. With the males and Interrecon, yes, we've shown it can work."

"What about enlisting Klethos, female or male, into the Marines? Or any human army?"

That threw her for a loop. Enlist Klethos into the Marines? Even if it could be done, there would be significant pushback within the human factions, only beginning with the Brotherhood. There were more who might accept Klethos help but balk at actually integrating the military.

If it worked, then it would certainly bind the Klethos to humanity. But could they manage to do it?

"If the Klethos would agree to it, then possibly, if we start with the males. I'm not sure the warriors would make good grunts. They have an aversion to taking orders, even from their own kind."

The chairman smiled, then leaned back. Sky realized that he'd been waiting for her opinion, and she guessed that she'd just confirmed what he'd already decided to do. What she didn't know was if this was a course of action that was already in the works, or if this was merely a Federation proposal.

"Thank you, Skylar, for your frank answers. I'd like you to do two things for me. First, as you attend the conference, feel out your fellows to see what they think about such an integration of forces. Maybe drop a few hints here and there and see what they say. Second, if you can, meet with the Klethos and see if this might even be a possibility with them. The quad will be attending the conference before they leave. See what they think.

"Can you do that?"

"Yes, sir, I can. I don't know what kind of reception I'll receive, but I can certainly broach the subject."

"Good, I knew I could count on you. And, you'd . . . *we* had . . . better get going. The opening ceremony is going to start soon. I'd like you to enter the hall with me, if you don't mind."

He held out one hand, indicating the office door. Sky preceded him out where her three escorts were waiting for them.

He was already playing politics. Entering the hall with him was a signal that she was someone of importance. That might help her do as he asked and determine how others might accept an integrated military with the Klethos.

She thought he was correct as well. They needed the Klethos, and the Klethos needed them. The Dictymorphs were not done with them. The alliance could not break up. Integrating the military forces was as good a way as any to make sure the alliance remained strong.

And if she had any say in it, she was going to make it happen.

OSIRIS

Chapter 28
Hondo

Amazing Grace, how sweet the sound,
That saved a wretch like me.
I once was lost but now am found,
Was blind, but now I see.

Hondo stared at the grass beneath his feet as the last strains of the hymn faded away. There was a quiet rustling as the gathered people looked up to where 24 M96's had been driven, muzzle-first, into the ground, a combat helmet covering each stock. Two boots were neatly aligned in front of each one. Hondo stared at them as the chaplain led the gathered Marines in prayer. He paused after the prayer, then started a short speech, making the usual comments about righteousness and sacrifice. Hondo didn't really listen. He'd heard the same speech too many times before.

The CG had done the fallen right by the setting, though. Hondo had attended Heroes Ceremonies in chapels and even a university auditorium, but never in an open field, lined by trees, and with mountains in the distance. It felt right.

Task Force Juarez had only been a part of the overall Marine mission on Osiris. Across the planet, other Heroes Ceremonies were being conducted. Including the 6,212 Marines that had been lost when their transport had been shot down, 23,759 Marines and sailors had been lost beyond resurrection. The number was staggering, and this was for a *victory*.

Every one of the Marines and sailors would have their names read aloud on the world for which they gave their lives. It was an honor given to them, and a reminder for those left behind. As long as their memories remained with the living, then they never really died.

Hondo had attended 2/17's Heroes Ceremony that morning, sitting quietly as 419 names were read. He only recognized three names: one had gone through boot camp with him at Camp Charles, and the other two had served with him over the years. But all were his brothers and sisters.

This ceremony hit him on a deeper level, however. This was for Charlie Battery. Technically, the ceremony was for the entire artillery battalion, but the only losses were in the battery. Hondo still felt responsible for his part in the fight and had to pay his respects.

Four Marines sat in the front row, the only Marines in the battery left on the planet. Six had been casevac'd off-planet. The remaining 24 were KIA.

Sitting next to him was Tabitha. The survivors of Petersford Landing were in a refugee camp, and on a whim, Hondo had contacted the mayor the night before, telling her about the ceremony. That morning, she'd arrived.

It had been good to see her, despite the circumstances. Ben had been casevac'd along with the rest of the WIAs the morning after the battle. Hondo had been essentially rudderless for the last week, with no mission, no command structure, and no partner. He'd had nothing but his thoughts, and that was not usually a good thing after a battle. He'd hugged it out with Tabitha, and if a few tears fell onto her shoulder, then that could be expected.

The chaplain sat down, and from the front row, the battalion commander—who'd flown in from the mission headquarters half-way around the planet—stood up and made pretty much the same remarks, adding that the fallen had not been lost in vain, but instead, that they had helped make the victory possible. He even pointed out Tabitha and mentioned how the battery had saved the survivors of the village.

Hondo had been surprised by that. He'd put that in his report, of course, but as far as he knew, no one had known that Tabitha would be there at the ceremony.

The CO finished his remarks, and the sergeant major stood up and moved to the front. Hondo didn't know how he was going to run this. There were two ways to conduct a Heroes Ceremony. One—which is what they had to have done with the Marines and sailors who'd been killed on the transport—was to simply have a reading of the names of the fallen, with two or three readers at a time, taking turns as the went down the list. The other was to have a symbolic roll call. Charlie Battery—as automated as it was—only had 33 Marines and a corpsman in the entire unit, far fewer than an infantry company. But with only four Marines present, that might make it awkward.

"Addison, Carter," the sergeant major said.

"Here, Sergeant Major," one of the four Marines answered.

Roll call it is.

"Adoud, Farouk."

"Absent, but accounted for," Sergeant Bianchi, the senior of the four Marines said.

Adoud must have been one of the Marines who'd been casevac'd.

"Belling, Claude."

Silence greeted him.

"Corporal Claude Belling."

Still nothing.

"Corporal Claude D. Belling," he said for a third time.

In a subdued voice, the sergeant major said, "Corporal Claude D. Belling, killed in action, July 19, 484, Osiris.

"Billingham, Laura."

"Absent, but accounted for," Bianchi replied.

The sergeant major continued down the battery roster, calling out the names. Most were announced as KIA.

Hondo only knew one name, and he tensed up when 2nd Lieutenant Barret Sung's name was called, then announced as KIA.

"Tiburon, Arabelle," the sergeant major intoned.

"Sergeant Arabelle K. G. Tiburon."

Hondo had never met the sergeant. She'd just been a voice on the other end of the comms. But through her, he'd been connected to the entire battery.

"Sergeant Arabelle K. G. Tiburon, killed in action, July 19, 484, Osiris."

The sergeant major went through the rest of the roster, ending with Lance Corporal Festus Wysoki, who stood up, arm in regen sleeve, and proudly said, "Here!" Normally, friends of the fallen might go forward to recount a few memories, but with only four survivors there, that might have been painful. So, it was a good place to end with Wysoki.

Some of the gathered people moved forward to have a word with the survivors, but Hondo didn't feel the need. Just being there was enough.

"So, they tell me you-all are about to leave," Tabitha said as they walked back to the temporary camp.

"There'll be a rear party hanging around for a while, but yeah, we're starting to leave in the morning. I'm scheduled to depart at 1330."

"Thank you. You and Ben," she told him.

He shrugged. He could have said something along the lines of "Just doing our jobs, ma'am." That was the trope, at least, said over countless Hollybolly flicks. But he wasn't a trope, so he said nothing.

"I've got something for you. For you and Ben, if you can give him his, too."

Hondo stopped, about to protest. It was against regulations for a Marine to take, or even receive, anything from a battle. The reg was designed to eliminate trophy-taking, but also to maintain good relations with the civilians they were sworn to protect.

Before he could refuse, she pressed two small rectangles into his hand.

"I can't . . ." he started before curiosity overcame him.

It won't hurt just to take a look, right?

He pushed the start, and a 3D of a lovely village appeared alongside a gently flowing river. Most of the homes were white with brown slant roofs, and mature evergreens graced the town.

"Petersford Landing?" he asked, already knowing the answer.

A face appeared at the top, that of a young girl, possibly eight years old.

"Thank you, Staff Sergeant McKeever, and thank you, Team Member Ben, for saving me. My name is Hinaa Quinn."

She said the words so carefully that he knew they'd been carefully rehearsed, but the moment she finished, she broke into a smile that was all her, that was genuine. Her image shrunk and flew to the top corner of the image. Another one appeared, this one of a teen boy who gave his own message before his image flew up to join Hinaa's.

One by one, each of the survivors expressed their thanks and appreciation. When Tabitha's image shrunk and flew up to the top, all 108 of their tiny images rang out with a unified "thank you." The images stayed: a patchwork quilt of humanity above the image of the village.

A 3D display like this could be bought at any store in human space for a few credits. Then it was just a matter of time to get everyone's recording. It wasn't worth much, but that didn't make it any less illegal. He couldn't accept it, and he couldn't take Ben's back for him.

But he sure appreciated the thought. He took another minute to simply look at it, watching the river flow by.

Screw it!

He slipped both of the loops into his cargo pocket.

Let them run NJP on me if they want. I'm keeping mine.

"Thank you, Tabitha. And please let everyone know that I love mine."

Tabitha pulled him into a hug and whispered into his ear, "If either of you ever gets a chance, come back and visit. We would love to see you both again."

Hondo had dropped tears on her shoulder that morning, and he did it again. But these tears were different. These were tears, not of joy, perhaps, but of relief, of satisfaction.

He had just sat through a Heroes Ceremony, mourning the loss of fellow Marines, but the goofy little 3D loop had reminded him why they had fought. Third Platoon hadn't hesitated to use four of their rounds on the Grubs surrounding the villagers. For him to mope around, feeling guilty, made light of their sacrifice. It diminished what they had done.

Marines—and soldiers, sailors, airmen, and coasties—existed to serve the people. Charlie Battery, First Battalion, Fiftieth Marines, had just joined a long, long line of those who'd answered the call of duty and made the ultimate sacrifice.

It wasn't called a "Heroes Ceremony" for nothing.

Over Tabitha's shoulder, he could still see the people at the ceremony site. He could still see the M96, helmet on top, stuck into the ground.

He gave the weapon a sloppy salute, still holding Tabitha's hug.

"Semper fi, Marines," he whispered.

FSS ULTIMATE VOYAGER

Chapter 29

Hondo

"Are you Staff Sergeant McKeever?" the corporal asked.

The corporal has just poked his head into the supply locker and seemed surprised to see him lounging on his makeshift rack.

"Yeah, that's me."

"You should be on your PA. The whole ship's looking for you."

"What for?" he asked with a sinking feeling in his gut.

Hondo was a loose end. He reported to no one on the ship, and he hadn't even been assigned a berthing space. That was OK with him. This was not a Navy ship, but rather, a commercial liner leased to move troops, and when he'd found out where housekeeping kept their blankets and sheets, that had been good enough for him. He set up a cot, outfitted it with what the placards proudly proclaimed to be 2400-count cotton sheets, and made his own private stateroom. He wasn't far from one of the galleys, and he had a head across the passage. He'd checked out a high-end reader from the ship's library and was enjoying the crossing by catching up on his reading.

"The chief of staff wants to see you, like right now, Staff Sergeant," he said, before saying into his PA, "I found him, Gunny. He was in one of the housekeeping storerooms."

"Do you know what this is about, Corporal?"

"Not a clue, Staff Sergeant, only that you've got to go now."

"OK, let me get dressed first," he said, pointing down to his skivvies, the only thing he had on at the moment.

"Oh, I just needed to find you. I'm not going to escort you to officer's country."

With that, the corporal ducked back out, leaving Hondo to wonder what was going on.

Only one way to find out.

He put on his utilities and checked himself in the small hand mirror he'd found in the corner along with some other personal items. His hand brushed the two gifts he'd accepted from Tabitha.

It can't be that, he told himself.

The chief of staff was the third senior Marine in the entire task force—that was Task Force Mexico, not the break-away Task Force Juarez. He was a brigadier general. Some staff sergeant accepting a gift from some civilians was far, far, below his paygrade.

Still, he took the displays and slipped them under the sheets on his cot before he left his "stateroom." Then he simply stood in the passage. He didn't know where officers' country was. This was a passenger liner, not a Navy ship. He had to stop and ask four people before he got directions and made his way to "Platinum Passage," the shipping line's term for the top class. He had to ask where the chief of staff's stateroom was, but he finally found his way and knocked on the edge of the open hatch.

"Come in," someone said.

Hondo stepped into the stateroom. The place was gorgeous, with what looked like real wood bulkheads (although Hondo was no expert—they could have been applications over the ship's structural bulkheads, for all he knew). The luxury was spoiled, though, by the eight Marines in the room and an entire communications suite, manned by a corporal. This may have been a commercial liner, but it was obvious that top brass were not relaxing.

"Who are you?" a colonel asked as he came in.

"Staff Sergeant Hondo McKeever, sir. I was told—"

"That will be all, gentlemen," the general said. "Take a break and come back in twenty. You, too, Corporal Farris."

Hondo was confused, so he reverted back to the non-rate self-defense mechanism when with an O. He just picked a spot on the bulkhead above and behind the general and stared at it.

"Just where the hell have you been, Staff Sergeant?" the general asked as soon as his stateroom was cleared.

"Nowhere, sir. I've just been reading."

"Nowhere? Why aren't you in the Staff NCOs quarters?"

"I wasn't on the billeting list, sir. So, I just made do."

"No billeting? See Master Guns Phoenix about that after we're done. So, now, as to why we've been looking for you, who do you know in the Office of the Chairman?"

"Sir? The Office of the Chairman?"

"That's what I said."

"Chairman?" Hondo repeated, completely confused.

"As in the Chairman of the United Federation." the general said, his eyes boring a hole into Hondo as if he could peel every layer to get at the truth.

Holy shit! What now?

"Sir, I don't know anyone!"

The general stood and stared at him as if trying to decide whether to believe him or not. Hondo shifted his gaze even higher on the bulkhead.

Hondo was not a recruit, and he was no longer in awe of an officer just because of the rank on his or her collar. But this was a general officer, and they could make life extremely difficult for a mere staff sergeant, should they so desire.

"Well, someone in the OOC sure knows you. They want me to set up a secure communications link for you, one that I won't be privy to."

He walked over to the comms suite, entered something on a physical keyboard, and studied it.

"Hmph. Looks like it's going in about 12 minutes. Either someone was standing by waiting for you, or we caught someone at the right time."

He looked back up at Hondo and asked, "This isn't some of that Interrecon sneaky shit, is it?"

"Not with the chairman, sir. We answer to the UAM, sir. Not the chairman."

"Maybe so, Staff Sergeant, but you won't be with Interrecon forever. Don't forget that. If the chairman wants something, you'd better well give it."

"Yes, sir, of course, sir."

"Well, I don't know what they want from you, and I guess I won't. This is beyond my clearance. Have you used a PYR-90 before?"

"No, sir."

"Then come here."

The general spent the next two minutes showing him how to operate it, which was not difficult at all. When the call came in, he'd scan his eyes, put his finger in the sleeve for a DNA match, then talk. That simple. The general acted as if he wanted to say something else, then shook his head. He told Hondo to secure the call when he was finished, then leave. He'd be waiting outside the hatch.

Hondo waited for the call, nervously chewing his fingernails. This was new territory for him; territory he didn't like.

He almost jumped out of his seat when the call came through. He looked into the retinal scan, then put his finger in the sleeve. A moment later, a thin, elderly man appeared on the screen. He looked vaguely familiar, but Hondo couldn't imagine from where.

"Staff Sergeant McKeever, thank you for taking this call."

As if I had a choice.

"I received the confirmation just as the vice-minister was returning, so if you can wait a moment, she'll be right in."

The man went back to his PA, made an entry, and pretty much ignored him.

This is freaking weird!

After only a minute, the man looked up and said to someone outside of the pickup, "Ma'am, I've got the Staff Sergeant here now."

"Now? OK, that's fine. I've got a few minutes."

Hondo recognized the woman who sat down in front of the pickup. It was Skylar Ybarra, the government scientist who he'd run into four times now. He didn't realize that she was so high up in the OOC, and he couldn't imagine what she would want with him.

"Staff Sergeant McKeever, thank you so much for your time. Do you remember who I am?"

"Yes, ma'am. Of course, I do."

"Good. And I've been following your career."

Junior Marines learned early on never to steer a conversation until they knew what was going on, but Hondo was so surprised by that comment, that he couldn't stop himself.

"Me? For God's sake, why?"

"Well, you saved my life three times now, so I'd think that was normal. That's why, when I saw you in Marine Recon, I had you transferred to Interrecon."

That's what happened? I wondered why I was chosen, he thought, a little pissed that anyone was manipulating his career.

"And that is why I wanted to speak to you now. But before I do, let me remind you that all of this is strictly confidential. You are not to mention this to anyone unless I give the OK."

"Even to the commandant? The chairman?"

"Yes, even to the commandant. The chairman, well, yes, of course you can talk to him if he reaches out to you."

Holy shit! The chairman might reach out to me? And if the commandant asks, I've got to say no?

Hondo was becoming extremely uncomfortable with the direction this conversation was taking.

"Look, Staff Sergeant. I don't have much time, so let me ask you straight. What is your opinion of the Klethos you've served with? Particularly Ben."

She knows a hell of a lot about me.

"Ma'am, the Klethos are good warriors, and Ben, he's a good guy."

"Good guy? So, is he a friend?"

Oh, fuck. Did I say something wrong? He was about to back off when he thought, *Screw it. I'm not going to worry about what she wants me to say.*

"Yes, ma'am. A friend. A good friend."

She nodded but otherwise kept her expression neutral.

"OK, then let me ask you this. You've worked with the normal Klethos units. You've worked with the male Klethos in Interrecon. How well do you think they meshed with the Marines?"

That was a trickier question, and Hondo instinctively knew that this was getting to her key question. He felt the same loyalty to his Klethos brothers and sisters as he would to anyone else with whom he'd been in combat, but he couldn't just gold plate everything with her. He had to tell her the truth.

"The regular units, I'm glad they are on our side, but they . . . they're good fighting *beside* us, not *with* us, if that makes any sense." He looked at her, but she hadn't changed her expression, so he continued. "The males, ma'am, they're different. Not as strong, nor as fierce, so that's a mark against them, but they're also more flexible. They aren't so worried about their honor. To be blunt, they aren't the dicks that the females are."

The vice-minister almost broke out into a laugh, and Hondo realized what he'd said: the females were "dicks,' while the males weren't. He'd just embarrassed himself and maybe insulted her.

"Oh, sorry ma'am. I didn't mean it that way."

She waved him off with a hand and said, "Crude and ironic, but your point is well-taken." She seemed to think about it for a moment, then asked, "So, let me give it to you straight. Given all that you know, given your experiences, do you think we could integrate the Klethos into the Marines?"

That stopped Hondo dead, and his mouth dropped open as he stared at her.

"Integrate?"

"As in bring them into the Corps, as Marines."

Marines? Make them Marines?

Hondo didn't know what to say. The thought had never crossed his mind. Sure, they had people from all over human space who enlisted, not just Federation citizens. But they were human, not aliens.

He stopped to consider her question, wondering how to put her off or talk around the issue, but then it hit him. He already knew the answer. He'd known it for a while even if he hadn't specifically posed the question to himself.

"The warrior Klethos, no, ma'am. We need them alongside of us, and I want them by my side, but they cannot accept the discipline to be part of a Marine squad. Give them a mission and let them complete it in their own way."

Does she look disappointed?

If she was, that wasn't going to change what he had to say.

"But the males? And females who aren't warrior cast—"

"Wait, what about females not in the warrior caste? What are you getting at?"

"Not all females are warriors, ma'am. You know that, right? The warriors we see, they're like the Amazons, the ones chosen to defend the rest. You know, the males, the children, the other females. Those females are still bigger and stronger than any human, and they're not such, well . . ."

"Dicks?"

Hondo felt his face turning red, but he said, "Yes, ma'am. What I was saying, though, was that the males and the rest, they're more understanding, more adaptive. They could serve as Marines."

She sat there, just looking at him. A voice said something from beyond the pickup, and she waved and said, "OK, Keyshon. Just one more second," before returning her attention to Hondo. "I've got to go. I might want to talk to you again, possibly here on Earth. So, one more question, then I'll let you go.

"If it was up to you, would you want to have Ben serving with you as a Federation Marine?"

There was only one answer he could give to that, and he wasn't going to pretty it up for her.

"You better fucking believe it, ma'am!"

EARTH

Chapter 30
Sky

"Thank you for meeting me, Gary," Sky said to the male member of the liaison Quad.

"Of course, I would come. You are *d'lamma*," he replied.

I really need to find out what that means, she noted, knowing she could search later to try and find the meaning. Glinda had called her that two years before, as well.

"So, when are you leaving us? I mean, your Quad."

"When the time has come, we will have left."

Sometimes, the Klethos were clear as day in their wording, but sometimes she couldn't make heads nor tails of what they meant. Sky didn't know what Gary meant by that. It could be that he just didn't want to answer. As far as humans could tell, the concept of lying was not as well-developedfor Klethos as it was for humans, and this could simply be a way to subvert the question.

It doesn't matter. That was just small talk. Better to just get to the point.

"Gary, with the withdrawal of the Dictymorphs from sixty-three of your worlds, we have what looks like an unbroken boundary between the world you hold now and the ones they hold."

"This is true."

"And on the other side of you are the worlds held by humankind."

"This is true, as well."

Sky looked for any of the tells that humans had been able to identify in the Klethos, but Gary was showing nothing.

You'd be a good poker player, my friend.

"We humans, we would like to know what you're going to do about the Dictymorphs. We know they still hold many of the worlds you lost to them."

"We will do as we must."

Which tells me nothing.

Rumor was that the Quad would be leaving tomorrow, and Sky needed to get some sort of answer from him. She couldn't rely on the give-and-take she'd been taught by the chairman's own political advisor, Dr. Beachcroft.

Well, I've gone contrary to my coaches before, and that seemed to work out OK.

"Gary, to be blunt, the Dictymorphs have pulled back, and we are concerned that any renewed hostilities could result in a full-scale galactic war—one that neither of our peoples are prepared for."

There was the tiniest flicker of the tips of his two leftmost neck fronds.

Bingo! I've hit a nerve of some sort. Keep it up.

"We need time to build up our forces, you need time, but most of all, we need to work together."

OK, just say it.

"Some of us feel that not all Klethos consider humans *d'lato*. You came to us when there was no other option for your very survival, but now that the Dictymorphs have withdrawn, some of you wish to cut all contact with us and pursue a war on your own."

This time, the flicker in his frill was greater, with more fronds twitching.

"We believe this would be a grave mistake."

When Gary didn't say anything, Sky prompted, "Can you confirm or deny what I have said?"

"You are *d'lato*, that has been proven. It may be, to some of us, that we are not."

Whatever Sky had thought were possible responses, that wasn't one of them.

"I . . . I'm afraid I don't understand."

"And this is a problem. If you, Vice-Minister, do not understand us, then who among you can?"

"I understand honor, I understand '*d'lato*,' but no, I don't understand you now."

Gary stared at her for along moment, his neck frill flat against his upper shoulders. He had evidently regained control over his emotions.

"For more than a hundred of your years, our *d'relles* met your gladiators in the ring. Have you ever wondered why we allowed this?"

"Because of honor. We met you as warriors."

"First you met us with your combat suits. Later, you met our *d'relles* with genetically-modified fighters. And we permitted this, even when we could have destroyed your people as we have so many others."

We might not have been so easy to destroy, she thought, but kept that to herself.

"Yet, we allowed it. We enjoyed our relationship with you because—as you might put it—it was fun. It gave us pleasure to watch you keep trying. You humans gravitate to the underdog, as you say it. We are not so different in that."

This was a new concept, one she'd have to digest later. They fought in the ring for entertainment? They thought it fun to watch "underdogs" try and play with the big girls?

"So, why did you come to us for help, if we were so incapable?"

"Now, you are coming to understand. Either we misjudged you, dismissing your true capabilities until we needed you, or we dishonored ourselves by asking children, if I may use the term, to save us. Either way, it is a grave loss of honor."

It all fell into place. Either option would be a loss of honor to the Klethos, one they would have to right, and by pulling back, they would incur no more dishonor until they could rectify the wrong.

"How many of you think this way?"

"Enough. Most."

Sky's heart fell when she heard that. If the entire Klethos population felt like that, then what could she say to change their minds? Not much, she thought.

"Do you feel the same?"

"Yes, I am Klethos-lee, after all. But, I am willing to accept whatever is necessary to save my people."

Sky felt a surge of hope, and she asked, "Are there others like you?"

"Enough. Some."

Sky paused, trying to marshal her thoughts.

"If we split now, then coming back together will be difficult. We need to keep our connection."

Gary said nothing, so she pushed on with, "If there was some way—within honor—to remain at least partially connected, would you be willing to pursue it?"

"If we could maintain honor, then yes. As you say, that would make it easier once we have sorted ourselves out on the issue. Is this a hypothetical, or are you proposing something specific?"

"We need to keep the alliance alive, and the best way to do that is a marriage."

"Vice-Minister, we do not—"

"Sorry, bad choice of words. We need to integrate our people. We've already started this on a very small scale, but we can expand on it. Interrecon. We have humans and Klethos in the same unit, and it has worked surprisingly well. It has had none of the problems associated with our earlier attempts at integrating Klethos warriors into human units."

"And you wish to continue this?"

"Expand it, Gary. We want Klethos, male and non-fighter females to join our Marines, our Legion, our armies."

"Females? But not our fighters?"

"Your warriors are unparalleled fighters, but they can be d . . .difficult," she said, almost repeating what Staff Sergeant McKeever had said about them. "The males integrated with humans without problems, and we believe a large portion of your females could, too. Just not your fighting units. Let those who can enlist in our militaries. Let them live and fight when necessary. That would require a Quad, don't you think, to remain here? And that would keep the alliance alive."

She was wording it poorly, she knew, and she wished she were a better speaker. She knew this was the right move, and later, the alliance could deepen once the Klethos leadership got over their honor snit. She only hoped that Gary could see it, too.

"As always, Vice-Minister, you surprise me. This is something that we had not considered, nor even envisioned. I want to object, but I cannot find a logical reason to do so."

"So, you'll do it?" she asked.

"I cannot tell you yes or no. This must be discussed."

"But you will champion it?"

"I am but a servant of my people, not a champion, but yes, I will support the concept."

"If I can ask, what do you think the chances are that we can do this?" she asked, dreading the answer.

"Good," he said. "With small numbers of males—"

"Or other females."

"That might take longer. Males have always been the exceptions. For non-fighting females, that might take more time. But I think we might be able to provide four eights to join your military."

Sky did a quick calculation. The Klethos used a base eight system, and "four eights" was eight to the fourth, or 4,096 new recruits. That was not as many as she had envisioned, but it was a start.

"When do you think I will know?" she asked, mentally forming a list of what she would have to do on the human side to push the idea through.

"I will return in two hours to let you know."

What?

"Two hours?"

"Yes, it will take that long. I am sorry I cannot give you an answer now."

Holy crap! I'm just supposed to see if they would be conducive to the idea. No one has approved it on our side yet. Nor even debated it.

She swallowed hard, then said, "No problem. Take your time, and I will wait for your answer."

"You have proven again, Vice-Minister, that you're truly are *d'lamma*," Gary said before turning and leaving her office.

She stared at the door for a long moment before she voiced to her PA, "Get me the chairman now, priority alpha."

Sky had two hours to somehow put into place a major interspecies program, and she didn't have any time to waste.

PROPHESY

Epilogue
Hondo

"Come over here, Ben, and let me look at you," Hondo said.

Corporal KMC-1, United Federation Marine Corps, pulled at his dress blues collar with his organic upper hand, looking uncomfortable.

Join the club, Hondo thought. *No one ever has been comfortable in their blues—even if we look killer wicked.*

The Klethos Marines were adjusting well, but they were not particularly concerned with their uniforms, no matter how much grief the DIs had given them. It had evolved into one of the growing-pain issues that just had to be accepted. That didn't mean that Hondo was going to accept anything less today. He gave his friend the once-over, straightening up his ribbon bar on his right chest and the single medal on his left.

Compared to Hondo's line of medals—especially with his Navy Cross—Ben's single Purple Heart seemed an understatement, especially given what they'd accomplished together. But all of that was still classified. Technically, Ben shouldn't even have his Purple Heart. He had not been a Marine when he'd lost his hand, but a call to Vice-Minister Ybarra—who had headed the enlistment of Klethos into the Marines—had resulted in grandfathering in both time-in-service and some awards for those Interrecon Klethos who had then gone on to enlist in the Corps.

Ben reached up and brushed Hondo's new gunnery sergeant's chevrons. He'd been a gunny now for five months, but this was the first time since then that he'd been in his blues.

"I do not understand why you are doing this," Ben remarked. "It is not logical."

"Ha! Well, if it makes you feel any better, I sometimes question myself about it, too. Maybe you Klethos have it right. Well, not you guys being second-class citizens and all."

Ben lifted his upper arms in a Klethos-shrug, then said, "It is our way."

Cara poked her head into the room, took a second look, and then said, "Wow! That's two fine-looking Marines. But if you are done preening, it's time."

Hondo looked at Ben and said, "Let's do it!"

Ben held up his right upper hand, and the two fist-bumped, making a clanging noise as their prosthetics hit each other. Ben seemed to take great pleasure in fist-bumping Hondo at the slightest excuse.

Hondo had plenty of time to go through regen since the battle on Osiris, but he kept putting off the medical staff with one excuse after another. And then when Ben had returned with a camouflaged-pattern fake hand as well, it didn't seem right for him to go it alone. Human medical researchers were working to perfect Klethos regeneration, but until they did, the five serving Klethos who had lost limbs—or in one case, half of a face and neck frill—were stuck with prosthetics—prosthetics that were not nearly as functional as those made for humans.

It could be a sense of unity with his friend, and he was sure there was some of that, but Hondo simply felt comfortable with his hand. He'd even turned down the offer to "socialize" it, getting it covered with an artificial layer of flesh that looked and felt like real flesh to anyone else. He liked the camouflaged look, and he didn't feel a reason to hide it.

Ben left the room first as if he were Hondo's protector, clearing the way of lurking enemies. But there were no enemies here, just friends waiting as he entered the main hall.

BK saw him first, then stood up and gave him a tight hug, whispering into his ear, "Looking good, Hondo. Almost enough to make me want to take a taste myself."

Hondo felt his face redden and he laughed to cover his embarrassment. He tried to come up with a smart remark, but he had nothing. BK let him go.

Other friends caught his eye, mouthing well wishes and giving him thumbs-up: Tammy Pickerul, in her new sergeant's stripes, Wolf, Doc Leach, Tony B, Roy Rutledge, and Byron Howell, all the way from the Confederation. He was surprised to see Burger—no, Second Lieutenant Robert Hanaburgh now, not "Burger" any longer. He was still in school and hadn't thought he could make it.

They were his friends, his brothers and sisters in arms, and it meant so much to him that they had come. So many others, however, couldn't come. They were his brothers and sisters who had fallen in battle. Sam Gelhorn, Gary Callen, Lorenzo Marasco. First Sergeant Nordstrand. Lieutenant Abrams. And so many more, fellow Marines and corpsmen who sometimes visited him in his dreams.

Hondo had often wondered why he'd been spared when others had not. What had he done to deserve survival? But that kind of thinking could take someone down the rabbit hole. Lieutenant Abrams, who had done so much for his Marines, had been so tormented with his inner demons that he'd taken his own life. Hondo was alive, and so were the rest of those gathered here today. They had to accept that, take joy in it, and never forget the others who had fallen.

Chances were, more of them would fall. There hadn't been a Grub attack since Osiris, but they were out there. No one thought humans and Klethos had seen the last of them, and when they did come, as they surely would, more Marines would make the ultimate sacrifice.

Hell, snap out of it, McKeever! This isn't the time for melancholy introspection.

He and Ben reached the front and took their positions. Across from him, Cara gave him a slow wink, then broke out into a huge smile. That helped settle him down, and he looked back down the aisle with growing anticipation.

The music started, and Ben reached over to softly clink hands. A sigh swept through the crowd as Lauren, looking radiantly beautiful in her white dress, appeared in the back of the hall on the arm of her father, who looked regal and proud in his Navy dress whites.

His breath caught in his throat when Lauren caught his eyes, and her smile broadened into something more intimate, just for him.

Ben might not understand why humans married, but it was all part of life. Military men and women throughout the ages had witnessed humanity at its very worst, they had seen—and done—horrendous acts of savagery. Whether for good or bad, that affected every person who had answered the call to combat. But they'd also seen mankind at its very best. Men and women through the ages who had made the ultimate sacrifice for others.

Being in the military was giving all for others.

And life went on. Each man and woman had to grasp all that life had to offer. If not for marriage, families, gathering with friends, then what was the purpose of fighting?

Hondo was proud of being a Marine, and he could think of no other life. The Corps gave him purpose. But there was also room in his life for more: for love. The chances were that he would go into combat again, and he might not survive that. So right now, he had to grab at whatever he could.

And as Lauren walked down the aisle, her eyes locked on him, he was looking forward to embracing whatever the future brought to them both.

Thank you for reading *Division of Power*. I hope you enjoyed this book, and I welcome a review on Amazon, Goodreads, or any other outlet.

If you would like updates on new books releases, news, or special offers, please consider signing up for my mailing list. Your email will not be sold, rented, or in any other way disseminated. If you are interested, please sign up at the link below:

http://eepurl.com/bnFSHH

Other Books by Jonathan Brazee

The United Federation Marine Corps' Lysander Twins

Legacy Marines
Esther's Story: Recon Marine
Noah's Story: Marine Tanker
Esther's Story: Special Duty
Blood United

Coda

The United Federation Marine Corps

Recruit
Sergeant
Lieutenant
Captain
Major
Lieutenant Colonel
Colonel
Commandant

Rebel
(Set in the UFMC universe.)

Behind Enemy Lines
(A UFMC Prequel)

Women of the United Federation Marine Corps

Gladiator
Sniper
Corpsman

High Value Target (A Gracie Medicine Crow Short Story)
BOLO Mission (A Gracie Medicine Crow Short Story)
Weaponized Math

The United Federation Marine Corps' Grub Wars

Alliance
The Price of Honor
Division of Power

The Return of the Marines Trilogy

The Few
The Proud
The Marines

The Al Anbar Chronicles: First Marine Expeditionary Force--Iraq

Prisoner of Fallujah
Combat Corpsman
Sniper

Werewolf of Marines

Werewolf of Marines: Semper Lycanus
Werewolf of Marines: Patria Lycanus

Werewolf of Marines: Pax Lycanus

To The Shores of Tripoli

Wererat

Darwin's Quest: The Search for the Ultimate Survivor

Venus: A Paleolithic Short Story

Secession

Duty

Non-Fiction

Exercise for a Longer Life

Author Website
http://www.jonathanbrazee.com